Soul Transplants

Bruce Alway

Millions, maybe Billions, of people around the world believe that everyone possesses an eternal soul.

So, what is the soul?
The Individual's Will, Emotions, Mind, and Power.

Other books by the author:
Our Ghost Family
These Afflicted Minds
Two Unlikely Romances
Genieous!
New Poems and More Wisdom

BruceAlway23@gmail.com Soul Transplants © 2017

The First Soul Transplant

Mrs. Tyler, a middle school teacher and native of Seattle, was present. She is in her late forties and on life support. According to her legal directive, she had received her dying grandfather's soul. With doctors standing back from her hospital bed in a private recovery room, the anesthesiologist announced, "She should be coming out of anesthesia soon."

Moments later, the patient awoke. Her wide eyes shifted in confusion. Dr. Morgan stepped to the side of the bed. "How are you feeling, Mrs. Tyler?

The patient, whose gaze had become distant, suddenly focused on him. Mrs. Tyler reached up, grabbed the doctor's neck weakly, and gritted her teeth.

"Pa said I'd find you out here, Sheriff. Surprised ya, didn't I? Heard ya has been lookin' fer me. Ain't no one gonna hang me–not you, not no one! Now, yer gonna die."

Dr. Morgan easily pried her frail hands off his neck and requested soft restraints. Mrs. Tyler weakly tried to break free from the soft restraints, spoke in French, then fell back and gasped. Her wide eyes stared blankly, her body went limp, and she stopped breathing. The heart monitor flatlined, and the oxygen alarm sounded. A doctor issued commands for an injection.

"She's in defib," a nurse exclaimed. The top of her hospital gown was thrown open, and the defibrillator paddles were placed on her chest.

"Clear!" Mrs. Taylor's body heaved slightly, and the doctor quickly glanced at the EKG monitor, which started to show a faint rhythm.

"We got her back," a nurse declared.

Mrs. Tyler opened her sleepy eyes and drowsily asked in her usual voice, "Where am I? Where are my husband and children?"

The heart monitor alarm sounded again. Dr. Morgan ordered, "Clear!"

Her body heaved slightly once more. The patient's eyes widened in terror, and she mumbled something resembling an ancient dialect of

Celtic as she weakly struggled against the restraints. The monitor flat-lined again as Mrs. Tyler lay still.

"One more time! Clear!" The third shock was in vain. Dr. Morgan sighed. "Dammit! We did everything we could. I'm calling it – 2:47 PM." He looked down at her with compassion. "I'm sorry, Joyce." Dr. Andrews stepped away from the gurney, shook his head, and exited the room.

<u>One Month Earlier – The First Committee Meeting</u>

U.S. Marshals discreetly escorted nine professionals wearing lanyards around their necks who displayed their I.D.s to a secure underground parking area in a building guarded by security personnel. An armed guard led each committee member from the private garage.

Inside the conference room, water pitchers and empty glasses rested on the table in front of each black leather chair. Microphones were evenly spaced along the length of the table. Seated in the chairs were the appointed committee members, including medical doctors, experts, religious leaders, lawyers, judges, and scientists, all of whom were ready for the first meeting. At the same time, two armed guards stood outside the closed door.

Dr. Morgan, the committee chair, approached the podium as Mr. Sanchez, sitting next to the podium, activated the video and audio recorders. "Ladies and gentlemen, although most of you know me, for the record, my name is Dr. Sydney Morgan. Thank you for accommodating your busy schedules to serve on this monthly committee. Remember that you were hand-selected for this committee to contribute your questions, thoughts, expertise, theories, and general assistance in guiding us forward. You understand its parameters, as each of you has received top-secret clearance.

Dr. Morgan continued by inviting all members to introduce themselves and share their professions and areas of expertise. "Here are some of the ground rules. These meetings, interviews, sessions, and surgeries will be video-recorded for accountability and posterity. I must remind you of the gravity and confidentiality of every aspect of this new endeavor. Therefore, there must be no discussion with anyone outside this room or any other meetings in which you are present, not even among ourselves. The forms you signed pledged this secrecy. Please do not take any notes. Mr. Sanchez or I will contact you when we need to speak with you outside this room. I ask that you talk into the microphone nearest you when you have a question or comment.

The first point on the agenda is to review some recent events. To assist with this, I would like to introduce Mr. Sanchez, our Committee Secretary and Chief Record Keeper for the project. Mr. Sanchez has a wide range of responsibilities, including videotaping, taking minutes, gathering and organizing reports and interviews, documenting research, collecting medical records, coordinating activities, and performing other essential tasks. Thank you, Mr. Sanchez.

We have named this effort The Soul Transplants Project, or STP for short. Since we lack a better term for this recently discovered energy, we are using the common term 'soul' to describe it. It seems to fit. Until recently, we couldn't even prove the existence of what is commonly called the soul.

Dr. Lee raised his hand. "Doctor, are we sure that what you found is a 'soul'? That's quite a claim."

"Medically and scientifically speaking," Dr. Morgan replied. "It can't be anything else. It's not like anything else. Mr. Sanchez has a few images from the scope."

Mr. Sanchez tapped the keys on his laptop as Dr. Morgan stepped over to the wall-mounted screen and pointed to an image displaying the light blue hue inside a human body lying on an operating table. "As you can see, the life energy is mostly concentrated around the brain and extends to the spinal cord."

The committee members leaned forward with fascination as they considered agreeing with the idea. At the same time, each felt excited, convinced that this image represented a human soul.

"Next, we have the video, Dr. Morgan said." As the video played, Dr. Morgan continued, "This is a close-up of the life energy, as close as the scope could get. Notice the colorful strands swimming and the short flares that extend and retract in the blue ring." Dr. Morgan smiled and spread his hands. "Let me just freeze-frame this for a moment. Ladies,

3

gentlemen, and colleagues, we have discovered the soul. What other discovery in all of history can compare to this one? Let me sum up the answer with one word: none. Not the pyramids, the atom, or black holes. That which has been talked about for thousands of years and believed in by cultures throughout the history of humanity has now been proven to exist." The committee responded with smiles and soft clapping as Dr. Morgan continued, "Even though the discovery was accidental, it takes nothing from it. Many discoveries have been made."

One of the committee members raised a hand. "Dr. Morgan, is the soul just life energy, or can there be something else?"

"Just life energy, as far as we can tell. I sincerely hope that's all there is to it."

"How were you able to see this?" Dr. Doyle asked.

"So basically, Dr. Carol Brown, sitting here, developed an experimental imaging technology to better see inside the human body. I was with my team using it one day and began making adjustments. That's when we saw this life energy."

Mr. Sanchez interrupted from his seat, smiling. "For a long time, he had known Dr. Morgan and wanted to give the modest doctor his rightful place in history. "Doctor, wasn't it you who first saw it?"

"Well, yes, but of course, the credit goes to Dr. Brown and my team. We were all there. However, it's an amazing feeling and a privilege to be the first human to lay eyes upon a discovery of this unprecedented size and significance. Our progress to date is that we have detected the human soul with advanced imagery and have spent millions of dollars and a lot of time developing the technology to remove souls from a few terminally ill patients who have donated their bodies and souls to science. Scientifically speaking, the good news is that a few souls have already been carefully extracted and stored in a special version of an incubator; however, the souls have since disappeared. Nothing much was left at that point, at least anything we could determine. Perhaps the soul is similar to a physical organ in that neither can be sustained outside the body for an extended period. Of course, the extraction immediately terminates the donor's life. The current challenges are that we can't measure, dissect, or weigh the soul.

4

We don't know if the soul has a form of DNA or some other unique kind of code. I hope it doesn't. I hope the soul is pure 'life energy,' the spark and source of human life. We know many things about the human body and the mind, but at this point, we know nothing about the formation of the soul, its evolution, or its composition. This technology is uncharted territory waiting to be understood, and that's our purpose." Dr. Morgan became animated. "Folks, this is huge. I'm excited to be with you on the front edge of this technology. Since the soul appears to be 'life energy' or possibly human life itself, the theory and hope are that a soul can be extracted from a terminal donor and placed into a recipient who has just passed or is on life support. Its energy could fire up the neurons, bring subjects back to life, and even restore the mind! In the most basic terms, one might think of it as jumping a dead battery in a car. Imagine resurrecting the dead! Of course, if we were successful, 'resurrecting the dead' must be added to the Hippocratic Oath." Gentle laughter filled the room. "As always, are there any comments or questions from the committee?"

"Dr. Morgan, as a representative of the religious community, I have moral and spiritual concerns. Perhaps my role on this committee is to monitor developments from that perspective. I suspect that the traditionally accepted parameters of life, death, and the soul may need to be reconsidered or even face threats."

"Thank you, Reverend Doctor. Let me address these valid concerns. So far, we have determined that the soul is energy, but not that it includes other components. At the very least, it is the energy of human life, and it might only be that – we hope it's just that. However, if the soul is too complex or unique to understand, then this energy might be personal, meaning specific to the individual, like a fingerprint, and cannot be transplanted. As for the soul being of a spiritual nature, I'm not sure if we will ever be able to determine that, although we all understand and respect any religious position."

The Reverend continued, "Dr. Morgan, lastly, let me say that so far, I'm not opposed to the direction of this new science. If the medical and scientific communities can give life back to the deceased, and there is nothing more than that, I find nothing wrong. Further, I applaud it. I remember reading a story in the Bible about a man raised from the dead long ago." Careful laughter lightened the mood in the room. "However, it's the belief of many religions that the soul is a person's essence, containing the mind, will, emotions, and power, and it's a person's soul that goes to heaven. If this science intends to separate the life energy from the personal signature and transplant the life energy, then I'm a fan." The Reverend's demeanor became very serious and stern as she added, "But if a transplant can't be done seamlessly or if this concern is not regarded as this science moves forward, you can expect an international shouting mob of religions with torches to gather at your castle's door, and I'll be the one in front holding the pitchfork."

Dr. Morgan tried to maintain his enthusiastic demeanor by quickly adding, "I agree. To our credit, Reverend, we are already giving life back to people in a sense. For example, we can often restart a patient whose heart has stopped with an electrical shock. We also harvest and transplant organs from people who have died and place the organs into the living to give them the chance to live again. I know that bodies and souls are different, but I just wanted to state that."

Most of the room silently agreed that the body and soul were not comparable in the doctor's response. Nevertheless, they understood the analogy.

"Are there any other comments or questions? Yes, Dr. Garcia."

"Dr. Morgan, if the soul is the product of the merging of the human sperm and egg, then is anyone from the S.T.P. taking a closer look at human reproduction, specifically, conception?"

"That's a great question, Dr. Garcia. The answer is 'yes.' We have a team of specialists working to trace the process backward from adults to human embryos to determine at which stage of human development energy becomes detectable and whether this energy increases or changes as individuals mature. These studies are moving slowly because there isn't exactly a line of volunteers. The legal branch of the Soul Transplant program, led by Judge Green, who is sitting here with us, faces the challenge of acquiring consent from volunteers without disclosing the complete reason for the procedure or the underlying science.

Some aspects of this study aim to investigate whether sperm and eggs have their own energies and, if so, what occurs to these energies at the moment of conception? As with any new technological breakthrough of a sensitive nature, concerns always arise. We are progressing cautiously and slowly as if we are carefully crossing a frozen pond without knowing the thickness of the ice. I maintain a mindset of cautious optimism, as I believe we all do. The keyword here is optimism. Are there any further questions or comments from the committee?

"Dr. Morgan. I have one."

"Yes, Dr. Doyle."

"Dr. Morgan, we have successfully harvested a soul and transplanted it into the new high-level technology incubator, but what tests have been conducted to determine if the receiving patient will accept the soul?"

"Dr. Doyle, the transplants of human souls into recently deceased pigs, cows, and horses were disappointing. There was obvious evidence that a transplant had been made, perhaps fully or partially, but the test animals subsequently rejected it. However, something did happen. The immediate responses were, at the very least, unsettling. The experiments with these animals concluded that they were incompatible with humans. They all displayed vital signs after the transplant. Every animal died after a few moments of panic and hysteria, except for Autumn, the chimpanzee. The staff witnessed, moments after coming out of anesthesia, she spoke in muddled distress, "I'm dying. Don't let me die. Please, no!" They also heard the word "cancer" within her normal chimp sounds in her fear. We'll play the video to see how that progresses. The possibilities are emerging, and they seem to align with our initial goals, even at this early stage. But I must warn you that what you are about to see is disturbing.

Mr. Sanchez tapped a sequence of keys on his laptop as Dr. Morgan walked over to the room's light switch near the door and dimmed the lights. Everyone's attention was fixed on the screen. Some committee members sat wide-eyed while others covered their mouths as scenes of various recently deceased animals on life support were

7

displayed on a table infused with human souls. Some of the smaller test animals jolted once before dying, while others thrashed violently before going limp. Some writhed fiercely, seemingly terrified. The segment featuring Autumn was eerie and terrifying. Some committee members were still wiping away tears even after the video ended. A few sipped from their water glasses and cleared their throats. The lights were turned back on as quiet comments from the committee subsided.

"Dr. Morgan, did the chimp have cancer?" one specialist asked in a subdued tone.

"No, Doctor. But the human donor did. Autopsies were performed, and the cause of death was determined to be a General Traumatic Shock. Animals aren't exactly like humans, but the experiment only aimed to determine whether a transplant could be completed. The good news about that experiment is that the animals were dead and came back to some degree of life, however briefly, but she talked."

Dr. Morgan stepped out from behind the podium, looked at the committee with delight, and said with controlled enthusiasm, "Ladies and gentlemen, let's not just give a passing glance to this historic moment. Something happened to those dead animals. Something did happen. Some human souls were transplanted, allowing them to return to life for a brief period. We're heading in the right direction. We have some traction. We have something quantifiable."

Most members nodded and smiled at his enthusiasm. Dr. Brown initiated a brief but weak round of applause.

Dr. Morgan, since we have the funding, the legal basis, and the technology, how soon can we begin the first human soul transplant?

"Well, Dr. Thomas, that's also good news. We must begin the first transplant very soon. As we speak, a father has less than a month to live and wants to give his soul to his daughter, who has just been placed on Life Support. She died suddenly after a mysterious illness. Ladies and gentlemen, we need to try this. I don't see it as a 'damned if you do and damned if you don't' situation. It's a 'damned if we don't at least try to give life back,' right? We're still walking on the frozen pond, and the ice hasn't cracked yet. We have already chosen an

8

undisclosed medical facility and date. The medical and psychiatric teams have been selected; some are sitting with us. Is there anything else? Yes, Dr. Andrews.

"Yeah." Dr. Andrews appeared upset, staring at the empty water glass before he began to speak in a slow, deliberate tone. "I've been debating with myself about saying anything, but I finally decided that I couldn't keep quiet, that I shouldn't keep quiet. I want to err on the side of extreme caution. Although I'm also interested in and support this new technology and its potential benefits, many essential questions need to be addressed. Some of these questions have already been asked, but they seem to circulate around this project." The doctor stood up and slowly walked around the conference table. He spoke with an urgent tone, clearly agitated. "We're talking about people... However, most of these discussions focus on the clinical aspects, technology, and science. What precisely is being transplanted? We're calling it a soul, but what the hell is it exactly? Where did it come from? Damn, it could be alien or supernatural, for all we know! Even as scientists, maybe we have finally found the line we shouldn't cross."

"Is there such a line?" Dr. Brown asked in disbelief as if he hadn't heard her question.

Dr. Andrews continued, "Or, maybe the soul is from God, as probably most people believe! What will the initial impact be on the recipient, and what will the short- and long-term risks be? I know - we won't know the answers, unfortunately, until we do these transplants. I hope we're not handling human souls like damn gallbladders! It feels like a group of children with matches trespassing into a wheat field on a windy day!"

A few heads gently nodded. Dr. Andrews returned to his chair and sank into his seat. He fumbled with the water pitcher, overfilled his glass, and took a quick drink before trying to clean up the spilled water with his handkerchief. "I'm sorry. This pursuit has made me a little emotional and given me great pause."

"Dr. Andrews, there is no need to apologize," Dr. Morgan replied. "You wouldn't be a good scientist or human if you didn't get emotional sometimes. And you're right; this is huge. I want to assure you and

9

everyone else that we are proceeding with great care and addressing these concerns at every step. Are there any other questions or comments?" He waited a moment. "No? I thank you all again. Some of us have a plane to catch. We'll see you next month." The group began to stand.

"Dr. Morgan, I would like to be excused from this committee effective immediately. I don't want to be involved in this. I won't have my name associated with the SP." Everyone froze where they were.

Dr. Andrews, please, we need your expertise. As a scientist, I know you want to see what the technology and research will produce, and then you can reconsider afterward. Help us steer. We need your hand on the wheel. Remember, once someone is removed from the committee, they will no longer have any further access to the SP. Would you consider staying on until after the first transplant? Is this acceptable?

Dr. Andrews sighed. "Yes. I'll at least do that much."

"Let me thank you on behalf of the committee," Dr. Morgan responded.

Dr. Morgan concluded the meeting since there were no further questions. "Thank you, ladies and gentlemen. See you next time."

Mr. Sanchez knocked on the door, informing the guard that the meeting had ended. The guard unlocked the door and radioed ahead. In two minutes, a line of security personnel arrived to escort the waiting committee members back to the parking area in the same manner they had been brought in.

The Second Committee Meeting

The committee members paired up in various locations around the conference room to talk.

"Ladies and gentlemen, please take your seats, and then we can begin," Dr. Morgan announced as he stepped up to the podium. The members stopped their conversations and took their seats.

"First, I'll give you an update. The first soul transplant was not completely successful. Unfortunately, the patient, Mrs. Tyler, died from shock during recovery after speaking in different accents. However, there was a transfer. Incomplete? It seems so. It could have been as minor as not precisely tuning one of the many dials, or the timing between stages could have been incorrect. Perhaps the electrical current was an issue. However, scientifically speaking, since there was sufficient evidence of at least some part of a transplant, we are investigating what went wrong and plan to proceed with another transplant."

"Damn right," Dr. Brown said with a tone of 'obviously.' "Listen, all the great inventors had a trail of failures behind them, and the explorers got lost and wandered before they found what they were looking for. Men die in battle before the army wins the war. Science is no different. We learn and plod on."

The room was silent as the other team members noticed the ease with which Dr. Brown glided past the tragic death. But what was more troubling was her indifferent tone.

"We want to be careful that we don't think about Mrs. Tyler as a disposable specimen," Dr. Morgan replied. "Or a simple by-product of our unsteady hand."

We understand, Doctor Morgan. However, the patient was terminal and was going to die soon anyway.

Dr. Morgan replied sharply, "That has nothing to do with it. You're not getting it. Or, maybe you and I place a different value on life, one that our science just took!"

Dr. Brown was clearly annoyed as she nervously bit her lip and stared at him. She wanted to continue but recognized that Dr. Morgan was the head of the committee and could dismiss her.

"Moving on," Dr. Morgan said, "we have found more terminally ill volunteers who have chosen to donate their souls to a family member on life support." Dr. Morgan smiled as he looked at a middle-aged woman, shaking his head in disapproval. "Judge, I can't even imagine the number of legal forms designated for that." The levity was well received as the team gently laughed. The judge rolled her eyes and smiled.

"Mr. Sanchez, is there anything else?" Dr. Morgan asked.

I don't have any updates. I'm just sitting here, thinking about a young woman on life support and hoping for the best. Her name is Julie.

"Yes. As we all are. Thank you all. See you here at our next meeting."

The Second Soul Transplant

Each family member had already said their sad goodbyes at Cathy's house before she and her mother, Helen, were taken in an unmarked ambulance to the airport and ultimately flown to the undisclosed hospital where Helen lay in her bed. Dr. Morgan turned to leave the private room.

"I'll leave you two ladies for a couple of minutes so you can talk. As we discussed, I want to remind you that the procedure will be recorded." He reached down and took Helen's hand. "Helen, on a personal note, the world would be a better place if there were more people like you, and if this procedure goes the way we think it will, the world will be a better place because of you. Goodbye." Dr. Morgan left the room, and the two women were left alone.

"Are you sure you want to do this, Mom?" Cathy asked, standing beside the hospital bed and holding her mother's hand.

"Yes, Cathy, I'm positive. I never had a doubt. I'm going to die soon anyway, and my dead sixteen-year-old granddaughter is down the hall. It's just the machines keeping her body alive. The damn seizure came from nowhere. Cathy, have you ever wondered where you will be when you die and how you will die? What if you could give your life instead of having it taken from you by some disease or letting old age just run its course? Old age isn't fun, Cathy. I don't want it said of me that 'she died an old lady who finally succumbed to congestive heart failure.' I want to be known as the woman who gave her life to her dead granddaughter so she could have the long and full life she deserves. I'm ecstatic about this privilege. Besides, even if the procedure doesn't work, I'll be in heaven with Julie."

Cathy was silent for a moment before she spoke. "Thank you." She bent over and kissed her mom. "I'm proud to be your daughter, and

12

Julie will always be thankful for what you did for her. She will always have some of her grandmother, Helen, with her."

Dr. Morgan and another doctor walked into the room and respectfully announced, "Helen, it's time. Are you two ready?"

"Ready and happy to do it, Dr. Morgan," she replied with as much strength as she could muster.

"Good. Julie is already in the O.R., Cathy, and it's time for you to go to the observation room. You can watch from there. Some of the machines are blocked from your view for security purposes. You'll be able to see your daughter and mother."

"I understand," Cathy replied.

As Helen was being wheeled into the operating room, she lifted her head to see her granddaughter lying unconscious, surrounded by tubes, computers, and various machines making their sounds. Helen was positioned on the other side of a large machine and managed to wave to her daughter through the observation window. Cathy blew a kiss back to her mom, tears streaming down her cheeks as she held a tissue under her nose.

"Helen, you're a saint. We all voted, and it was unanimous, so it's official," the nurse said from behind her mask.

"I'm not a saint. I'm a grandmother."

There's not much of a difference if you ask me. As I explained, I will put this mask over your mouth, and you count out loud to twenty. So long, sweet angel.

Helen closed her eyes and began counting. The numbers faded: "1 2 3... 4... 5... 6....... 7...."

As Cathy watched from the window, the mechanical arm of the machine between the beds was carefully guided over her mom's body by three technicians. It reminded her of a crane that picks something up, swings over, and places it back down. Switches flipped up, knobs adjusted, and rubber-gloved fingers tapped on computer keyboards. Like a neon sign, a glowing cone slowly extended downward from the mechanical arm and stopped above her mom's body. It flickered a few times, paused, and withdrew back up. The slowly bouncing line on

13

Helen's heart machine lay flat with a long warning beep. Cathy heard the faint sound and cried. Her mother was dead.

"Nurse, I gave clear instructions for the volume to be turned off on that monitor," Dr. Morgan said sternly.

"I'm sorry, doctor."

A technician looked up from her keyboard. "Doctor, we have extracted the donor's soul."

A light-blue cloud-like form appeared in the magnified transparent incubator on the mechanical arm. Tiny colorful threads seemed to be swimming inside it.

Dr. Morgan replied, "You all know what to do now."

Most of the staff walked over to Julie's bed. Each of them knew exactly where to stand and what to do as the arm of the machine moved to her bed and stopped over her still body. The cone reached just above her chest and flickered as the light-blue energy was evacuated from the incubation chamber. Julie's body flinched as her grandmother's soul was introduced into her body, and the mechanical arm was raised and pulled away.

Another technician announced, "Doctor, the soul has been introduced into the recipient."

"What's the patient's name?" Dr. Morgan prodded.

"It's Julie, Doctor."

"Good. Always know their names."

"Yes, Doctor."

"Begin the shut-down procedure," Dr. Morgan ordered.

Some of the nurses stared at the monitors while the rest of the staff observed Julie as the life support machines were turned off one by one. The heart monitor indicated that her heart was beating on its own. Dr. Morgan turned to Cathy and twisted two fingers together for hope and good luck. He then returned to place his ear over Julie's mouth to ensure she was breathing independently, and he confirmed a heartbeat with his stethoscope. Once more, he looked to the window and gave Cathy a 'thumbs up.' Cathy mouthed, "Thank you," as she cradled her face in her hands. Julie was alive and breathing on her own with a healthy heartbeat.

Five days later, after being continually observed and tested extensively, Julie went home with her mom and a doctor, who brought his suitcase, several boxes, and a video camera.

The Third Committee Meeting

In the hall, the armed guard closed the doors and stood there.

Dr. Morgan started the meeting. "Ladies and gentlemen, please take your seats. We have a lot to cover. Regrettably, with so many people involved in the S.T.P., someone slipped out to the media, and you all know, as does the whole world. Mr. Sanchez receives numerous questions and inquiries about technology from around the world, a few of which he can address. But I'm still smiling all the time because the procedure to transplant a soul from one person to another was a success. Julie is off life support and back home with her family, having received a new gift from her dear grandmother. Due to our success, do you have any questions or comments for the committee? Dr. Hasashi, I see your raised hand."

"Dr. Morgan, have there been any side effects at all – anything unusual about Julie's health or behavior?"

"I'll ask Dr. Martin to answer your question. He's been staying with the family. Dr. Martin?"

The doctor gave the update from his chair. "Unfortunately, the answer is yes. Julie's health is fine. However, she is expressing some erratic thoughts, confusion, and anxiety at times. Her mother reports that Julie is asking many questions about her deceased relatives and has a new interest in her ancestry and geography."

Dr. Hasashi noted, "That doesn't seem so bad at this stage."

"There's more," Dr. Martin continued. "At times, I have detected slight foreign accents in her speech. Julie now wears long-sleeved dresses that reach down to her feet. Sometimes, she speaks broken Hebrew, although she wasn't taught the language and is not Jewish. Her appetite is healthy, but her food preferences are changing – she is requesting food from different parts of the world."

Unnoticed to all, the Reverend bowed her head slightly and closed her eyes.

Dr. Mattu offered, "We expect, as with a physical organ transplant, it will take time for her to accept and adjust to her new life energy completely."

Dr. Martin concluded, "We continue to monitor her progress closely and have other doctors rotating in to stay with the family in their guest room to video record and monitor her."

Dr. Morgan said, "Let's hope she quickly adapts to the life energy. Does anyone else have a question or thought?" He looked around the table and waited. "No? Okay. I want us to continue to remain optimistic. Like any other new field of science, this one is exciting, mysterious, and sometimes uncertain. Some have accused us of 'playing God.' I've been called 'Dr. Frankenstein.' This is a science, and I trust it will allow some people who have died to live again as it develops. That's why I'm in this. This is what it's all about. We are the harbingers, ladies and gentlemen! We are in the same league as the early explorers and the first man to walk on the moon. Finally, we have received the go-ahead for the third and fourth transplants, which we will perform shortly. The case is similar to the others in that the donor is terminal, and the benefactor is on life support.

"I want to thank everyone here for your courage and tenacity," Dr. Brown said. "And for staying the course. Someday, our names will be enshrined in history. But, more importantly, a science that will one day save lives and possibly create better people."

Dr. Morgan kept his gaze on her even after she finished speaking, then addressed the committee, "Thank you again for your time and dedication. I want to thank Dr. Andrews for agreeing to remain on the committee. See you all next time."

The Third Soul Transplant

Twenty-five-year-old Mike Swanson lay in his private, guarded hospital room, just coming out of anesthesia. He slowly opened his eyes and saw the nurse beside his bed.

"I'm alive," he said in a half-whisper before he looked at the doctor, who was standing at the end of his bed. "Who are you?"

16

Dr. Morgan walked over to stand by Mike's side. "Mike, I'm Dr. Morgan. Yes, you were alive again. You had a Sudden Cardiac Death. Mike, I have some good and bad news to share with you. The good news is you're alive again because your father donated something very precious and important to you – his soul."

"What? I'm not getting this."

"Mike… your parents were in a car accident. They were on their way to visit you last evening and to decide about discontinuing your life support. Your mom walked away from the crash with a broken arm and some bumps and scratches. The responders rushed your father here by helicopter. Your dad didn't survive. I'm sorry."

"My dad is dead, but I'm alive?"

Dr. Morgan replied, "I'm very sorry, Mike. You're alive, thanks to your father, who loved you enough to include giving you his soul in his living will."

"Oh, my God… my dad is gone," Mike sobbed.

"I'm sorry, son." Dr. Morgan placed his hand on Mike's shoulder.

"For having the transplant just this morning, you're doing very well," the nurse awkwardly said, hoping to redirect his attention. "So, Mike, physically, how are you feeling?"

"Honestly, I feel tired, sad, and weird, but I guess that's to be expected."

"Weird, how?" the nurse asked.

"I don't know how to explain it, but it feels like my dad is very close to me."

"Do you think it's just a strong emotional connection?"

Mike shrugged his shoulders. "Maybe it is. Dad and I were always good buddies. He was a fast-talking, fun kind of guy. We did many things together, and he was my best friend. But I feel like it might be more than that - like he's right here with me."

The nurse rolled her eyes, put her hands on her hips, and smiled. "Mike, just be prepared for more scans and tests."

"I'll schedule a specialist to come and talk to you about what you're feeling," Dr. Morgan said.

"Hooray, examinations," Mike flatly replied. The nurse winked at him, and they both forced a smile.

Julie's Ancestors Crowd Her Out

Cathy sat nervously in the hospital waiting room, rapidly flipping through magazines while psychiatrists and specialists spoke with Julie in the conference room just down the hall. She wondered why police officers were stationed at every elevator and one outside the room where she was waiting.

After a few minutes, Dr. Morgan left the conference room and entered the waiting area. When Cathy saw him, she instantly tossed the magazine onto the table and stood up.

"Cathy, your daughter has permitted you to be in the room. We don't usually allow this, but we agreed that you must be included in this circumstance. I need to prepare you; it's a little disturbing. Please follow me."

Dr. Morgan led her down the hall and stopped before opening the door. "Cathy, we're video recording this session. We will have you sit in the empty chair on the side, a little off to the side of the group. And no disrespect; I realize you're her mom, but please refrain from speaking unless we invite you to join the discussion. It's a very delicate situation."

Through her emotional tension, she replied, "Yes, I understand."

The carpeted Consultation Room was comfortable, and the wallpaper, plants, and pictures added warmth, creating a cozy atmosphere that resembled a living room. Several professional men and women sat expressionless yet attentively with clipboards and pens on their laps. Some wore lab coats with stethoscopes around their necks, while others donned business suits.

Cathy gazed at her daughter, who wore an old-fashioned dress, as she walked to her chair. She reached out to her daughter with a trembling hand but withdrew it cautiously.

Julie noticed her mother's hand move. "Hello, ma'am. Pleased to meet you," she said with a subtle accent, avoiding direct eye contact with her mother. She never called her mother 'ma'am.'

Dr. Morgan began the discussion. "The reason for this special session is that Julie was suspended from school for being disruptive and saying inappropriate things to some students and faculty. Julie, I would like you to tell us about your day again if you would please."

Julie said nothing, so Dr. Morgan leaned forward and made eye contact. "Would you please tell us about your day in school?"

Julie's head moved slowly as her eyes flickered erratically, failing to focus on anything. "Just like I said, it was much ado about nothin'. I was talkin' to the teacher about how times are changin' so fast, ya know. Children don't hardly use their manners no more these days, n' ladies wearin' men's clothes, 'n boys holdin' hands with other boys like they were a girl. The teacher fetched the nurse, who took me to the principal's office, and they sent word to my ma. She came n' fetched me and brought me here… I told the principal I know where a lot of gold is buried in Arizona."

"How do you know this?" a psychiatrist asked. It seemed to the specialists, quietly sitting, that Julie might have Dissociative Identity Disorder or erratic and fragmented memories, which could have been triggered by something related to the new life energy Julie had been given. They didn't know that parts of her ancestors' souls had been activated. The result was clear as crowded personalities vied for expression within Julie.

"B'cuz I remember buryin' it, and I marked the spot. I told him I'd give him a cut if he helped me fetch it. He said he didn't think my act was cute, but it weren't no act at all. I reckon he didn't believe me that I robbed the stage. I could take you there … if'n ya let me outta here… ain't nothin' but a week's ride." Her speech slowed. "I recollect… something… I think it's… Arizona."

"Are you an outlaw?"

Julie's thoughts were scattered. "I believe… I think I recollect…that folks call me Wild… Joe. That's what's on the wanted posters. Five hundred dollars, dead or alive. They must want me perty bad. There's a poster of me too… Have ya seen it? It was afore I shaved off my beard."

She stopped talking and leaned forward in her chair, staring blankly as her accent and persona shifted to an old British dialect, her voice dropping to a low tone. "I remembuh killin' that bloody fool."

Tears ran down Julie's mother's cheeks as she quietly fumbled through her purse to find a fresh tissue while Dr. Morgan calmly asked, "Who did you kill?"

Julie sat back and continued searching for her past. In her normal voice, she answered, "I think I can recall doing it… It coulda been a dream… I can see it all in my mind." Her breathing became deep and rapid before her accent changed again. "E stole from me; 'e did. Five shillings… I cut the mate's throat that night, threw his body overboard, and watched it fall into the sea. Caught the damned fool alone on deck, I did, so I came up behind, real quiet, and hit hard on the back of his 'ead with a board. No more beatins' ell give me!" Her speech became dreamy. "The moonlight sparklin' on the top of the waves, the sails slappin' at the wind, the ship moanin' as it was slowly rockin'. No one eard the splash."

Julie's head tilted as her accent changed again. "Sergeant, we killed us some Injuns today, didn't we!" Her voice slowed. "I was there …wasn't I? Was that me, Sergeant? Did I do it? I can't seem to recollect very well. I'm old now." Julie grasped the arms of her chair and slowly rose to her feet. Panic filled her voice, and her eyes searched the distance and reached her arms as if she were blind.

"Mommy! Where are you?! I don't want Grandma's soul anymore! I don't know who I am! Get it out of me! I'm trapped with them! Make them go away! I hate them!" Julie stiffened and shouted, "Take this, you rebellious colonist bastards!" She raised an invisible musket and pulled back its invisible hammer. Julie swayed and collapsed to the floor, unconscious.

Two doctors jumped from their seats to assist her. "She's unconscious. Get the crash cart! stat!" Dr. Morgan ordered as another doctor rushed out the door.

Cathy stood up, extended her arms, and cried, "Oh, my God! Julie! I'm right here, sweetie. Mommy is right here."

The police officer outside the door entered the room and quickly ushered Cathy out, his arm around her shoulder, as she twisted her head back to look at the chaotic scene. "Come with me, ma'am. Let the doctors handle it."

The Final Committee Meeting

Mr. Sanchez started the audio and video recordings as Dr. Morgan began, lacking his usual enthusiasm for a football coach. His voice was slow and subdued.

"Ladies and gentlemen, thank you for coming. You know some things we must share, but we'll review everything to ensure clarity. First, Mr. Sanchez, please give us an update."

Mr. Sanchez stepped up to the podium. "Folks, the Soul Transplants Project has been issued a cease-and-desist order from the government effective immediately."

Dr. Morgan interrupted, "And I don't blame them. It was on my recommendation as the chairperson."

"Damn it!" Dr. Brown burst out. "Just because we haven't gotten everything all ironed out yet doesn't mean we should stop with this science! There are endless possibilities here! Don't you get it?!"

Dr. Morgan replied, "I strongly disagree, and so do the others here. We have discovered that the human soul is too complex to be fully comprehended. We didn't know that the soul's life energy included family history. It's that simple. We ruined four lives. It would seem unconscionable to any doctor to keep staggering forward."

"Ladies and gentlemen," Dr. Brown added passionately, "every great invention and breakthrough has had to go through these stages! It's just part of the path!"

Dr. Morgan quickly replied, "This path has ended at the edge of a cliff! And I won't push another life over the edge."

"Although there were some tragic and regretful incidents, there have always been such times in the history of medicine, technology, and science! Every pursuit is littered with debris and failures!" Dr. Brown replied.

The other committee members silently wondered if Dr. Brown realized that the term 'debris' wasn't the most appropriate way to describe the loss of human life. However, they would soon discover that her statement was close to what she genuinely believed and would eventually reveal the kind of person she was.

"Doctor Brown, it's over! We're done!"

The volume of Dr. Morgan's voice hushed the room for a few moments until Mr. Sanchez cleared his throat. "Although we tried our best to keep things under wraps, there were a few minor leaks, just enough to keep the media going. Some politicians are trying to distance themselves from the stand and have been forced to explain why they voted for it while assuring their constituents that they have sealed the lid on what they're calling 'Pandora's Box.' Since the S.T.P. had been classified as "top secret," all the information had been securely impounded, and our government still refuses to share any details about it. Funding has been reduced, but we can develop only specific parts of the science under stringent and guarded parameters. There are to be no more soul extractions or transplants, none at all. However, despite receiving some negative press, we have also received numerous private congratulations from the scientific community. Most of this committee will be dissolved at the end of this meeting. On a personal note, I want to say that it was a pleasure to work with all of you, and I'm proud to have my name associated with the S.T.P. Back to you, Dr. Morgan."

Standing at the podium again, Dr. Morgan concluded. "I would like to share my final notes and thoughts for the video. Although all four souls were successfully transplanted, the results were: The first patient, Mrs. Tyler, died from shock in recovery after manifesting a couple of completely different people. Julie has been admitted to a psychiatric hospital and remains there sedated. You all saw the video of her experiencing vivid and realistic influences from some of her ancestors. Her family is demanding that her grandmother's soul be removed. Who could blame them? At this point, we can't do it. We don't even have the technology to try. The third patient, Mike

Swanson, remains alive but has his soul and his father, Bruce's, too. After extensive tests and an investigation, it was determined that Mike wasn't deceased at the time of the transplant. His brain activity was very faint and fading, and it was expected to stop within minutes, so in the interest of time, the father's soul was introduced. Needless to say, the person who made the determination has been terminated. Now, the recipient has his soul and his father's soul. It seems to be an acceptable kind of symbiotic arrangement. This is not a case of a split personality but rather two separate souls cohabiting. We don't think that the two souls can be separated from each other at this point because it seems like, essentially, they're entwining themselves together for reasons and ways we don't know. We're closely monitoring this situation to see what happens. Will the two souls eventually become a single soul? We don't know that yet, either. This question, along with many others, remains unanswered. After the fourth transplant, Mr. Wilson, the recipient, went home. He hardly spoke to his wife, Karen, of fifteen years. In the rare times that he did speak, it sounded as if his wife said, "Like he was reading from a King James Bible." She complained that she had lost her happy husband. Three days later, he violently murdered the doctor who was staying with them and, moments later, murdered his wife. Afterward, he packed his bags and left. The authorities have been notified that he is at large, extremely dangerous, that he may seem confused and disoriented, and that he needs to be apprehended and taken to the nearest hospital."

Dr. Morgan sighed. A tone of regret was woven through the rest of his verbal report. "So, it turns out that the soul is more than just life energy. It appears to have a form of DNA that holds all the dormant memories, essence, and even some personalities from the family line. We suspect it dates back to prehistoric times, possibly even before. Likely, each new soul has the imprints of its ancestors; each new soul is layered over the imprints. Pardon the comparison, but the image of layers in an onion might help clarify the concept. In the case of the current technology, it seems that mostly bad memories, essences, and traits were activated from the history of the soul's gene pool, stimulated by the impatient, ambitious, and unstable hand of our new technology.

These awakenings are not dissimilar to documented cases where lightning strikes someone, or someone receives a severe blow to the head and instantly awakens with new musical abilities, knowledge of mathematics, or a foreign accent. Where did these new abilities come from? My guess is that the traumas were not just to the 'heads' of the victims, but the 'souls' too. These abilities were dislodged or activated from the victim's soul and somehow brought to the surface. Some ancestors must have been accomplished musicians or mathematicians, and those talents or knowledge were somehow awakened by trauma to the soul. On the positive side, I don't feel we should regret being part of it or apologize for it. The S.T.P. has made history, and hopefully, others in the future, like us, will take some of the technology forward more slowly and carefully to give the deceased new life. At that time, that group might have viewed our technology and tools as they would have viewed the tools of a battlefield surgeon during the Civil War. I suspect that some of this technology will be revisited now that we have laid the foundation. It may be revisited when the scientific community can understand the human soul more intimately and develop better technology to extract just the soul's life energy, if possible. Thank you so much for your contributions. Ladies and gentlemen, friends, and colleagues, it's been a sincere pleasure to have made history with you. Your drivers are waiting to take you back.

Dr. Brown stormed out of the room before the armed guards in the hallway could even open the doors. Most of the members felt that this wasn't over for her.

The F.B.I. is Directed to Apprehend a Dangerous Patient

Six rows of metal chairs were arranged in a curve, ensuring everyone could see the podium where an older man wore a dark suit and tie. Next to the podium, a large flat-screen TV, with Dr. Morgan seated beside it, was mounted on the wall. Outside the room, suited guards stood at both closed doors.

"Ladies and gentlemen, most of you know who I am. I'm Deputy Director Martin with the F.B.I. I need not remind you that this meeting is highly classified and strictly confidential, and we may be unable to answer some of your questions. I want to introduce you to Dr. Morgan. Dr. Morgan was the head of a top-secret scientific research project, and he needed our help. Doctor, please explain what you can, and tell us how we can help you."

Stepping over to the podium, Dr. Morgan began. "Thank you, Deputy Director. We need your help in finding and apprehending a male patient who is part of the voluntary experiment. I'm sure you have heard of the Soul Transplants Project. His name is Theodore Wilson. You have all been given a photograph of him, including his height, weight, hair color, and other details. There are at least three ways to identify him; one is by his appearance, which can naturally change slightly. Another way is by his fingerprints. The third, although broader, is his unusual behavior. Before Mr. Wilson left his middle-class home, without a word, he suddenly murdered the doctor who was staying in the home to observe him. Then, Mr. Wilson murdered his wife. Some of the violence was captured on the doctor's video camera. Please dim the lights. We want you to see the subject in a video so you'll better know what he looks like. The short video is disturbing at the least."

As the doctor recorded with a handheld video recorder, Mr. Wilson sat silently on the sofa.

"Mr. Wilson, you have hardly said anything since you came home. How are you feeling today?" the doctor asked.

Mr. Wilson stood and approached the doctor with a blank look. With a hidden knife he had taken from the kitchen, he stabbed the doctor several times in the chest. The doctor fell to the floor, gasping, and the video camera rolled to the floor, continuing to record the audio of the murder of his wife as she came from the kitchen, screaming, "Ted! No!"

Dr. Morgan pushed the button on the remote, and the screen turned black. "That's it. You can't identify him by his accent because we don't know what it will be. You won't be able to track him by his routines because they may change. This man might behave like a person with schizophrenia, or he might have just one personality. He might speak in an old French, Italian, or any other language dialect. He

25

could be anyone from any period in history. Due to these various possibilities, he cannot be accurately profiled. I'm sorry that I can't do better than that."

"He sounds like a seasoned spy - a master of disguises." The comment came from the group of seated agents.

"That might be a good comparison," the doctor replied. "In any case, he is to be considered extremely dangerous. Deputy Director Martin, back to you."

"All of you have the still frame picture of the subject in your packets. We know that after the murders, Mr. Wilson left his house in the family car. The description of that vehicle is in your folders, which I would like you to open and review the rules with me. Note that I used the word 'rules' and not the word 'guidelines,' so there is no room for subjectivity or need for interpretation. If you have questions, call your field supervisor, whom we will introduce shortly. They will be available by phone twenty-four hours a day. You all have copies in your folders, so follow along as I read the rules out loud. Number one - Under no circumstances is any of you to contact or question any of the subject's family members, neighbors, co-workers, or anyone else who might know him from before the murders. Number two - Do not contact anyone in other cooperating law enforcement agencies except for the names on your list. If you need to do this, it will be done with your Field Supervisor's prior knowledge and consent. You should never leave voice messages on your contact's phone or with anyone else. Number three - The public cannot be notified, and no press conferences or releases will exist. Number four – You should not discuss this assignment with anyone except your Field Supervisor. 'Anyone' includes co-workers, family, or social media. If you are assigned a partner, you will talk with them, but never in a public place. Number five – When the subject is apprehended, he cannot be arrested or charged. Just take him into custody and immediately call your supervisor. Number six – Do not use lethal force unless you or your partner is in extreme and imminent danger. You will all be assigned an E.I., or Electric Immobilizer, which, by our policy, is your first consideration in the event of necessary action. Number seven – You

26

must complete a daily report and submit it to your Field Supervisor and Mr. Sanchez, whom I'll introduce to you momentarily. Your Field Supervisor is privy to things that you can't know. Your Field Supervisor's name and number are in your folder. They are your go-to. All Field Supervisors will report to me at least daily. Number eight – When you arrive at your designated areas, call your Field Supervisor. I know some of these restrictions tie one of our hands behind our backs, but there are important reasons for this. We need to track the subject and find him. This hunt is a Priority-One manhunt. The U.S. Marshal Service is on standby for assistance if you feel the subject has been spotted, but again, call your Field Supervisor first. The contact names and numbers of all participating agencies are included in your folders and travel materials. Don't lose them. Dr. Morgan, do you have any final comments?"

"Yes, Deputy Director. The subject might visit museums or travel agencies. He could be seen at ethnic gatherings, where he may or may not appear to fit in, so be on the lookout for disruptions or anyone who looks out of place. He might visit libraries to read books on history, travel, or culture. He may use the internet at a library or visit an internet café to research his family tree or genealogy. If that makes sense, he will try to connect with something from the past, but not his past. That's all from me."

The Deputy Director continued, "You all will get a list of ethnic festivals and museum exhibits for the region you will be assigned to. Mr. Sanchez, agents will monitor every public computer in your respective areas and inform you of leads for anyone doing such searches. Do you have any questions for me or the doctor? No? A gentleman with a clipboard stands behind you at the back of the room. He is Mr. Sanchez. He has worked closely with us on past projects and will serve as the secretary for this assignment. Please give him your name; he will direct you to one of three tables where your Field Supervisor is waiting. Thank you."

The Shakespeare Play

Two F.B.I. agents in casual attire were assigned to observe the audience at the amphitheater in the city's park. Both agents had a picture of Mr. Wilson hidden in their programs.

Costumed actors performed on stage, skillfully exchanging their memorized lines. The curtain closed between scenes, allowing stagehands time to change the props.

After the performance ended, the agents who sat separately got up and walked around casually, blending in. Some of the audience gradually dispersed, while others talked among themselves and engaged with the costumed actors gathered in front of the stage for pictures and autographs.

Smiling, Mr. Abbot walked up to the lead actor. "Brilliant performance, my boy!" he exclaimed with a British accent.

"Thanks. We practice a lot," the actor replied in his American accent.

"You're not British?!" Mr. Abbot raised his voice in his old British accent, catching the attention of a nearby agent who casually moved toward the conversation.

"No. Most of us aren't British, but we all seem to have gotten the accent down pat. I believe a Shakespeare play shouldn't be performed in an American accent."

"You simply are imposters – all of you!"

The agent raised his arms as if adjusting his sunglasses and whispered into the radio concealed in his sleeve to summon the other agent, who promptly approached. The two agents stood a few feet behind the conversation, quietly discussing the play.

The actor became irritated and shot back, "Get real, buddy. It's a play performed in the U.S. What do you expect? Would you prefer the King to come here from England and perform?!"

Mr. Abbot raised his fist at the actor and shouted, "How dare you imply that His Majesty…"

The agents stepped in, showed their credentials, and seized Mr. Abbot's arms. "Sir, you will have to come with us."

"He's a jerk!" the actor barked.

Mr. Abbot twisted around violently, broke free from their grips, and ran through the remaining crowd, bumping into people, knocking over chairs, and entering the park. The agents quickly pursued him. One managed to pull out his cell phone and call his supervisor.

"This is Agent Pierson."

"What have you got, agent?" The voice on the phone asked.

Breathing heavily while running, the agent replied, "We think we got him! We're in foot pursuit! We just left the downtown park, and we're heading east!"

"I'll notify the Marshall Service. Don't lose him! Use your E.I. if you must. You must apprehend him!"

The agent stuffed his phone in his pocket.

The foot chase continued through the streets and between buildings until Mr. Abbot found himself in a dead-end alley. The two agents halted and slowly approached.

Agent Pierson said, "E.I." They both drew their E.I.s and aimed. "Mr. Abbot, don't move. We need to ask you some questions."

"You will not take me, you bloody bastards!"

Mr. Abbot reached for his gun and began to pull it out as both agents struck him with their E.I.s. Mr. Abbot convulsed for a moment before collapsing lifelessly to the ground. The agents jumped on him and cuffed his hands. They checked for vital signs and were relieved to discover he was breathing.

The agent called his supervisor again. Their supervisor answered, "Tell me, did you apprehend him?"

"Yes, we did."

"Tell me he's alive!" the supervisor demanded.

"He is. He drew a weapon. We used the E.I.s. We both did at the same time."

"Then we're damn lucky he's still alive. Give me your location. The Marshall Service or F.B.I. will be there in one minute."

"In one minute? That's pretty quick."

"Yes." The supervisor replied. "The FBI and the Marshal Service are positioned all over the city."

Mr. Wilson, Mr. Abbot, Mr. Wilson

The two agents who captured Mr. Abbot sat to the side in the ambulance as the doctors monitored him. He finally woke up, moaning, and spoke in his voice. "I feel like I've been hit by a truck. Where am I? What am I doing in an ambulance? Please call my wife. Is she okay?!"

"Just stay calm. What is your name, Sir?" Dr. Morgan asked as one of the agents videotaped.

The man answered, "Ted Wilson. It's Theodore."

"What is your wife's name?" the Doctor asked.

"Karen. Is she okay?"

Dr. Morgan instructed him, "Just rest, Mr. Wilson. All your questions will be answered later."

Mr. Wilson closed his eyes as he lay restrained on the gurney. His voice became quieter and slower as he struggled to explain. "It was like standing at the bottom of a deep pit, looking up at the narrow opening, and watching a movie about me as my mind was being... tapped. And voices... as if I were standing in the catacombs... The people were alive; some were quiet and resting, while others spoke loudly and argued... Their voices were blending and echoing. I knew some of them, dead relatives."

"Please just relax and rest, Mr. Wilson. I'll explain all of this after you are checked and get some sleep," Dr. Morgan assured.

The First Addendum to the S.T.P. Report

Dr. Morgan sat alone at his desk in his office, where he practiced and began typing on his laptop.

To whom it may concern,

I trust this addendum will be the last. Mr. Wilson, the final transplant patient, was apprehended. Of the four subjects who received a soul transplant, it seems he was transformed more than the others. He adopted the complete persona of one of his ancestors, Mr. Abbot, an assassin for the British Empire centuries ago, who appeared to draw on the experience and knowledge of modern society, as well as that of Mr.

Wilson. The government opted not to charge Mr. Wilson because they recognized that it was Mr. Abbot who aimed his gun at the agents.

Additionally, the government didn't want to face a trial that would expose them to public scrutiny. My head spins as I imagine what Mr. Wilson is experiencing. It seems that the combined electrical charge from the two Tasers caused Mr. Wilson to revert permanently to his usual self. Furthermore, Mrs. Taylor, the first test subject, appeared to switch personas in response to electrical shocks from the defibrillator. If the S.T.P. is reopened, this information should be investigated: specifically, how electrical charges and/or other stimuli can restore a subject to their original personality. Naturally, the follow-up question is whether controlled stimuli can toggle personas back and forth.

As with many new opportunities in culture, science, or medicine, there are efforts to push against traditional boundaries. If the potential of this new science reaches the general public, I envision cases of lovers requesting that their souls be placed in the same body, hoping for deeper intimacy. Other requests may come from family members asking for the souls of dying individuals to be transferred into their bodies to preserve their essence and relationships. However, the duration and extent to which multiple souls can coexist remain uncertain. There are already rumors suggesting that wealthy individuals exploit low-income families to essentially buy the young, healthy body of a volunteering family member so the soul of a rich, older, or dying person could be placed into the young, healthy body. This would allow the purchaser to live another life and perhaps even more beyond that.

Furthermore, what if the souls do not merge to form a single entity, or if one or both individuals find the relationship undesirable? Will science be able to separate them? Will one person seek legal avenues to claim the body and attempt to evict the other? What rights and choices will each possess? The questions and circumstances appear endless, not to mention the ethical and moral concerns involved. Truthfully, the scientist in me wants to continue exploring the soul and its mysterious power. Still, the human side of me believes we should leave it alone, allowing people to die naturally and letting their loved ones mourn their loss in a usual way. It is up to the next generation and those that follow, as I'm sure this topic will always remain a point of discussion in civilized society. Having served as the head cheerleader, I now gladly sign off on this addendum and the S.T.P. as it stands. Although I can never wash my hands of it, I hope and pray that the S.T.P. will be locked away in Pandora's Box, nailed shut, and not opened for a long, long time, if ever. My vote is 'never.' The soul is 'life energy' while hosting the personas of the family lineage. The soul is dominant, while the lineage is recessive—unless and until that order is disturbed. This disruption might contribute to some cases of Dissociative Identity Disorder, the belief held by some in reincarnation, or the mysterious sensation of déjà vu, as if being somewhere familiar, although never having been there before.

Finally, I would like to share some personal thoughts. My mind cannot find anything that compares to the soul. I feel a mix of fear and awe when I contemplate it. It is magnificent, mysterious, fantastic, possibly eternal, and largely beyond comprehension. The power of the soul seems ancient, yet every person born appears to possess a new and individual one. If nature alone created the soul, it stands as its most remarkable achievement. However, I believe the soul cannot be a product of evolution. If this is true, as I ponder the source, I look up at the night sky and gaze, overwhelmed by feelings of smallness and inadequacy.

Respectfully, Dr. Sidney Morgan

Former Chairman of the Soul Transplants Project

Two Years Later: Rescuing Julie

Dr. Morgan stood at the podium before the committee, half of whom were former members of the committee. Mr. Sanchez began the audio and video.

"Ladies and gentlemen, I never expected this to happen, but here we are again, revisiting the Soul Transplants Project. Some of you remember sitting in a room like this two years ago. Our mission this time is not to attempt to transplant a soul; rather, it is to separate the life energy from the family history within her soul. Now eighteen, she has been sedated and held in a psychiatric institution for the last two years. It took all this time to convince the government to allocate the funds to rescue Julie. Of course, we're thankful to Dr. Brown here, who seems to have some favor with the Senate budget committee."

Dr. Carol Brown wasn't driven by compassion. She had been privately lobbying senators for the past two years to advance the soul-science further. The chance to help Julie was merely a means to demonstrate the potential of advancing the science.

When a hand was raised, the specialist leaned closer to the microphone. "Dr. Morgan, what about the other two surviving recipients?"

"Yes," Dr. Morgan began. "Mike and his father opted not to undergo any more procedures to preserve the father's soul, and likely Mike's too. They understand that their situation is unique, and the simplest way to describe the results of their souls being together for two years is to think of conjoined twins who share major organs, including the brain. However, their cases are very different and complicated, so we can't predict the results. I'm glad they opted out because we don't have the technology and knowledge to ensure anything. They decided to, and I quote, "Live together and die together and let God sort things out when we get to heaven." It was fascinating speaking with them because I could tell when they talked. The father's voice had more energy and a slightly faster tempo than his son's, and their perspectives came from different generations. Although they occasionally have their differences, they get along just fine, and their love for each other is evident. Mike even jokes that they must do it when his father asks him to take out the garbage. I can't imagine the family issues regarding sleeping arrangements, etc. However, I do know that the mother/wife insists that each one identify themselves when speaking. Mr. Wilson also opted out. He remarried and hasn't had any further issues or manifestations, so they don't want to have the procedure done. He and his wife want to live everyday lives and be left alone, although Mr. Wilson agreed to a monthly examination.

There have been some good results with Julie regarding the administration of precisely controlled electrical shocks. In the tests, we reduced the medications, which caused stronger manifestations. We then performed the shock treatments, which, to some extent, subdued the manifestations. However, the therapy didn't yield satisfactory results, so her mother, Cathy, decided to allow Julie to undergo the procedure now that the extractor has been further developed. Our goal is to remove her soul, separate the life energy from its DNA imprints, and place her soul back into her with only life energy. Are there any comments or questions?

"Doctor Morgan, what if the procedure doesn't go as planned? What is the next step?" a doctor asked.

Cathy has authorized that her daughter will die with dignity in the operating room. In any case, the technology will be mothballed immediately after that.

In the hospital conference room, Dr. Morgan described the process to Cathy carefully and truthfully, "Cathy, these are the steps that will be taken in the procedure: First, we will extract Julie's soul. She will essentially die. Next, the extractor will, in simple terms, purify her soul, separating her life energy from her soul's DNA. Lastly, her soul will be reintroduced to her body with the expectation that it will be just 'Julie.'"

"What are the risks, doctor?" Cathy asked, teary-eyed.

"Cathy, I've always been honest with you. The risks include, in the worst case, her immediate death. There may also be unexpected results during the procedure. Our team is prepared to administer the necessary drugs to end her life with dignity. If she survives, she might not be able to have children. If she has children, they might die at birth or face any combination of issues. We don't know the consequences of a person being born without the family's soul line."

Julie arrived at the hospital in an unmarked ambulance and was placed in a secure room. The symptoms were severe and reminiscent of those in the conference room two years earlier. Battling for control, the conflicting personas reminded Dr. Morgan of the childhood game King of the Hill, where kids attempt to reach the top. However, in this situation, it was violent and potentially deadly.

A cacophony of voices and accents clamored to speak over one another, but one familiar voice sent shivers down Dr. Morgan's spine as he wheeled the gurney. It was Helen, Julie's grandmother. "Leave her alone!" she shouted to the other voices. "She is my granddaughter!"

Four patient assistants entered Julie's room, placed her on a hospital bed, and restrained her as she struggled against them. Various voices and accents threatened the staff while the personas within Julie cursed, threatened, and yelled. Dr. Morgan administered a sedative to Julie and waited for it to take effect. The volume of the voices diminished and eventually faded into silence. Her body relaxed as her eyes closed.

Once in the operating room, Julie was placed under the new but untested extractor. Her mother took her place in the viewing room and sat close to the window. The medical team stood tightly grouped around the latest machines in the middle of the operating room. A technician slowly pulled down the small lever. The extractor lowered itself, just touching Julie's body. A quiet buzz began as small buttons lit up one by one. Julie's heart monitor flatlined. Cathy had been here before and understood what was happening, but cried nonetheless. That was her baby girl lying there, and for at least a few moments, she was gone.

The gentle sounds and active lights indicated that something was happening inside. After thirty seconds, a nurse turned from her computer monitor and announced, "Doctor, we are ready for the countdown."

Dr. Morgan ordered, "Proceed on my mark… begin."

A mechanical voice from the computer began to count down from ten to one as a new set of sounds and lights were activated. When the computer voice finished the countdown, Julie's body jolted. A doctor restarted Julie's heart, which began to show activity. One by one, her vital signs were announced as expected. The staff completed their work, and Julie was wheeled to the Recovery Room.

Dr. Morgan pulled down his mask, smiled at Cathy, and gave his 'good luck' sign. Before joining the team, he ordered the technicians,

"Now turn that damn thing off, put it in storage, and lock the door."

"Yes, doctor."

Dr. Brown smiled excitedly behind her surgical mask. If successful, the separation would certainly enable her to move forward with secretly requesting funding from the Senate Finance Committee, and she would be in charge of everything.

The small group of senators standing comfortably around her would continue to let her disregard ethics and morals. All that the senators cared about was technology and success.

Dr. Morgan and Cathy gathered around Julie in the recovery room while the rest of the team stood back. Eventually, Julie struggled to open her eyes and let out a long moan. The tension was palpable; no one knew what was going to happen.

Dr. Morgan told Cathy, "Speak to your daughter."
Cathy leaned over Julie and said, "Baby, can you hear me?"
Julie spoke slowly, "Mommy? Is that you?" She opened her eyes and looked up at her mother, who began to cry. "Yes, it's me, Julie."

"How do you feel?"

Julie began to cry, too. Her mother kissed her on the cheek. Julie managed to say, "I feel tired and... peaceful. I think I'm better. I think they're all gone."

Second Addendum to STP Report

With a sigh of relief, Dr. Morgan entered the addendum while sitting at his desk.

To whom it may concern, I often find myself stating, 'this' is my last addendum to the Soul Transplants Project, but this one is indeed my final one. I'm pleased to write it as such. The new procedure was successful. Although Julie lost two precious years of her life—years that one could only try to imagine enduring—she has been restored to herself. To date, there are no signs of ancestral expressions.

36

In medical school, some suggest that doctors shouldn't get too close to their patients, meaning they shouldn't allow themselves to become too emotionally invested in their patients. Initially, I followed the advice and attempted to maintain a professional distance. However, after just a few years of practice, 'patients' turned into 'people.' As I walked with them through their arduous journeys, I grew close to some individuals, like Julie and her mother, Cathy. We have become friends and are teaming up against the STP.

I have suggested that we create a documentary or write a book about Julie's experiences when she is ready. She likes my idea for a title: "It's Us, Julie." We hope to raise awareness about the dangers of tampering with the soul and agree that experimentation on the human soul should cease. Yes, I used the word 'meddling.'

I'm glad this whole thing is over, at least for me. We learned a great deal of new science and developed advanced technology, but we also gained a deeper understanding of who we are as humans, even as more questions continued to pile up. I also gained a deeper understanding of a mother's love. Cathy rarely missed a day visiting her daughter in the institution, reading to her, talking to her, and sharing what was happening in the family. Always sedated, Julie couldn't speak, but her mother eventually sensed when she was talking to 'Julie' by the slightest changes in her eyes.

I sign off again as the chairman of the Soul Transplants Project and move on with great pleasure. I've heard rumors that science is secretly advancing after the recent success, and more funding has been allocated. Even if asked, I won't be involved again. This new science has already conflicted with my morals and ethics, as well as those of many people worldwide. God help us.

Sincerely, Dr. Sidney Morgan

The Senate Subcommittee

Dr. Morgan sat at the large wooden table behind a microphone in a small room of the Capitol building. It had been over three years since the Soul Transplants Project was last closed. He had been invited to speak as an expert to a confidential Senate Subcommittee regarding the advancement of S.T.P. technology. The senators were seated around the wide table.

The Chairperson, Senator Moseby, began. "Dr. Morgan, first of all, thank you for coming here to discuss the future of the Soul Transplants Project. You have been with it from its inception and have stayed with it throughout. Dr. Morgan, there is substantial pressure from a few sources to advance the SP. Historians, our military, and the medical and scientific communities are all interested in it. More than any others, our government is very focused on the SP. In your absence, technology has rapidly advanced. Scientists have mapped most of the soul's unique genome, providing greater abilities to manipulate the human soul. That last statement may not sound good, but that's where we are. Doctor, I'll get right to our goal. We aim to cultivate better humans - individuals with enhanced intelligence and a more enlightened perspective. We want to see the combination of the best characteristics from various soul imprints into a single person, to begin with, and then with other people if it goes well."

Dr. Morgan replied, "I wonder if it's a coincidence that your choice of words sounds awfully like those of one of my former colleagues, Dr. Carol Brown. Senator, why is that such an important goal? Why have computers and machines programmed people?"

The Chairperson paused before answering. "When it's said like that, it sounds terrible, and I must admit. Politically speaking, we have concluded that the reason why there is so much war, crime, and poverty in the world is that the Human Race, in its current state, can't manage itself or the planet we live on. We need higher intelligence - smarter people who can make better decisions. It's either this, or we continue to develop computers to make decisions for us, eventually becoming subjected to them."

Dr. Morgan pursed his lips and nodded his head slightly. "Modifying the genetics of the soul to produce superhumans, huh? My wife looked at me in a funny way when I told her that technology could lead to this. Genetically improved souls are what I'll call them, 'GIS' for short. Ladies and gentlemen, since you already seem to be on the threshold of doing this, why do you need me? I've been out of the loop for at least three years."

A different senator answered, "Because you are the face of The Soul Transplants Project."

"Did any of you read the book Julie and I wrote? Did you see that next to Julie's face is my face on the cover - 'faces of opposition'?"

"Yes, Doctor, we all read it. The book hit the top of every best-seller list."

Then you already know that I oppose further research and development. I'm sure Julie will join me and go public if necessary.

"Yes, we do know that," the chairman answered. But with these new humanitarian concerns, we hope you will lead the way in public relations. Doctor, we believe this is critical for the very survival of the human race."

Dr. Morgan looked around at the members. "So, you want more intelligent people to govern us? No disrespect, but we all do. I've already thought this through during many sleepless nights. Allow me to project the probabilities. You do see our form of government changing, then, don't you? Our proud and historical Republic will be replaced with an aristocracy, Marxism, totalitarianism, or an oligarchy. I'm looking at some of you, grinning in disbelief because you're sure that won't happen. But you can say goodbye to our three-party system, the Constitution, and the US Supreme Court. Again, some of you are still looking at me, and you don't think that will ever happen. So, this is what I foresee: First, this group of people with genetically improved souls, the GIS, will have small but impressive successes, followed by larger ones. They'll be elected to local political offices and make further improvements to their constituents' quality of life while promising additional benefits. To implement their innovative new policies, you'll ensure that one of these brilliant individuals becomes the President. That will occur before he tells us that to accomplish what needs to be done, there will have to be changes in our political structure and how our country operates. Of course, because nothing we've done up until then has worked well, we'll be open to any changes, as we desperately need him to lead us. However, we never contemplated his morals, ethics, or even his true goals. He'll tell us that the US Constitution must be amended, ignored, and deleted for him to continue, all while promising better results. Oh, there will be some resistance, the occasional uprising from newly formed citizen militias, and even a few attempts at a military coup, but they'll be squashed in time. Given his stellar track record of economic achievements, how could we not support this? Our states will end up ratifying the new changes because this guy is smarter than the rest of us and continues to assure us that he knows what he's doing and where he's going. But where is he going? He hasn't told us that yet. Some people won't like the attack on the Constitution and will demonstrate against it publicly, so our new GIS President enacts an indefinite martial law. Now, there is no going back. The GIS can't be stopped now and is much less opposed. Even with a mutated Constitution, the Supreme Court will attempt to rule against some of this new leader's activities and decisions. It doesn't matter because the court's decisions will be mostly ignored if the court hasn't already been dissolved by then. After all, our new leader is brilliant and will save us from ourselves. This GIS will rule the country without checks and balances because he fixes broken things and produces good results. We've never had it so good. Next, he offers assistance to other countries and promises vast improvements everywhere. Some citizens of that country initially resist but eventually embrace their new prosperity and appreciate their new 'advisor' appointed by our president. You guessed it - another GIS loyal to him. If any country resists him, our President applies his superior intelligence to military ambitions, along with the unlimited budget you've given him, and takes control, one nation at a time, until he rules them all under not our nation's flag but a new international one. Our stars and stripes are now hanging in the National Museum of US History, and it's illegal to display them publicly. Is this the scenario you'll settle for to ensure the human race survives? Senators, I'm not necessarily a religious man, but we could end up having the 'beast and dragon' kind of scenario from the book of Revelation - a fanatical view, perhaps, but one that many people will believe if one man rises to rule the nations. So, if you want to ensure the end of our country now and not allow our species to progress naturally, then tell our citizens right now just the part that you intend to create a GIS to rule them. He'll be a monster with all the best body parts to take away their rights, change their Constitution, remove their flag and freedom, and then watch a second Revolutionary War begin. You can add the other part about the one global government after the shooting ends; the prisons are filled with rebels, and the hospitals are overrun with the wounded and dying. Or, try to hide it all until the public catches wind of it and figures it out. Of course, another option is to halt the STP and research and development immediately.

Finally, the long silence from the committee ended as Senator Moseby spoke, "Dr. Morgan, we haven't thought it all out like that. As you say, we didn't 'project' the possibilities as you did, but I can imagine that a progression of events like that is possible. We saw a form of it in the Second World War." He looked around at the other members, "I, for one, will strongly suggest to the full committee that at least we do not continue to develop the technology of the Soul Transplants Project in this direction and shrink its financial allocation."

Most of the other subcommittee members nodded in agreement. However, the committee's response was deceptive. Most weren't convinced, as they had already been seduced by the promise of greater power. They had called the doctor to find out what he knew and assess his level of opposition.

"Thank you, Senators. You have done the best thing to preserve humanity – by preserving it. All of us would consider other ways to improve our world, and we're trying, but let's not forget to keep our hope in humanity. We are a relatively new species and are still trying to find our way in some areas. Even after all our mistakes, trips, and falls, we'll make it, starting with what we have learned and continuing to grow naturally."

Five Years Later

The government had publicly announced that the Soul Transplants Project was discontinued. However, under the leadership of Dr. Carol

41

Brown, they secretly continued working on the technology to create a better soul. Not even Dr. Morgan was aware of this.

Confidential volunteers become test subjects, as specific portions of human souls were extracted from donors and placed into the souls of the test subjects. Initially, there were tragic results as portions of the test subjects' souls were infused with the souls of the deceased. Some of them died in a way, as one witness described, "It was as if the subject was being electrocuted." Another female patient grew wide-eyed and then rapidly burst out names, information, languages, and events without the ability to stop. Quickly, she became exhausted and died on the table. Other subjects had internal meltdowns and became effectively brain-dead. Still, other test subjects survived and were taken to a secret location, but it was reported that they died during the procedure. The government did its best to cover up those tragedies. Finally, with the help of a few new drugs, the best test subject was produced and immediately brought forth to present to the public.

In Plain View

The rows of folding metal chairs on the grass were filled with people. The media were present and sat in front of the outdoor podium at the National Center for Science for a special announcement. Dr. Brown stood up from a line of seated guests at the back of the platform and stepped forward to the podium, smiling as Dr. Morgan sat in the audience, unnoticed, watching under his hat and sunglasses. She addressed the audience. "Ladies and gentlemen, press members, colleagues, and friends, welcome. My name is Dr. Carol Brown. We are excited to announce that, with new scientific advancements, we can more quickly advance the evolutionary process of the human species through the Advanced Soul Project, also known as 'ASP.' We have made extraordinary progress. Before introducing the first benefactor, I'll take just two questions from the media because we want to introduce the special man as soon as possible."

Dozens of hands were raised. Dr. Brown pointed to a reporter in the middle of the first row. The reporter stood.

"Dr. Brown, is the ASP a continuation of the Soul Transplant Project?"

"No, it is not. The project had shut down five years ago. The Advanced Soul Project stands on its merit, having conducted thorough research and developed its technology. Next question. You, right there in the brown jacket."

As the next reporter stood up to ask her a question, she was interrupted by the first one still on her feet. "Dr. Brown, but weren't you on the committee for the Soul Transplant?"

She dismissed his answer by saying, "Sir, you've asked your question, and now it's this person's turn." She turned to the second reporter and added, "Go ahead with your question."

"How is the ASP funded?"

Through private, confidential donations. Last question. You, right there."

"Dr. Brown, how is the patient, and what are the procedure's results?"

"The patient is doing very well. You'll meet him in a few moments. However, I will say this: he has been thoroughly tested. His IQ is well into the mid-two-hundred range. He speaks fourteen languages and is a living encyclopedia of history. Now, he is an accomplished pianist and can even start a fire without matches," Dr. Brown boasts.

Gentle and guarded laughter trembled throughout the seated audience. Dr. Brown extended her arm behind her to one of the individuals in the row of chairs. A man in his thirties stood up and walked to the podium to stand beside her.

"Ladies and gentlemen, please help me welcome Joshua Sims!" The audience clapped excitedly. Joshua stood carefully and walked to the podium. "Hello... Hallo...is salām 'Alaykum…Namaste…"

The audience laughs as Mr. Sims appears to showcase his knowledge of languages, yet he pushes on through the laughter, "My name is Lawrence…or maybe Sheila…. No, Major... I'm Gomez…. I'm from…I live in Sweden…. Canada… I'm Nigerian…"

The audience fell silent as Mr. Sims began to speak in various accents, his eyes distant and both hands pressed against the sides of his head. His body started to sway as he pretended to play an imaginary piano.

Dr. Brown tried to steady him and then glanced at the people behind her, saying, "We need some help here."

No one seemed to notice as a man in his mid-thirties walked up the three steps at the side of the platform. He pulled out a pistol, rushed over to Mr. Sims, and shot him twice in the chest before dropping the gun. He raised his hands, lay face down, and waited for the security guards to handcuff him. They stood him up and called the police. The frightened audience pushed their chairs aside and hurried back to their cars.

Police cars quickly filled the area. The assailant was transferred to the local police. The officer read him his rights while holding his small notebook. "Sir, what's your name?"

The man answered, "Mike Swanson." Then, in a different-sounding voice, he added, "And Bruce Swanson."

"Is Bruce your alias?"

"No. That's his name. 'Mike' is my name. I'm the dad, and he's my son. You need to contact Dr. Sydney Morgan. He's the guy in the green jacket near the podium arguing with Dr. Brown. It looks a bit heated."

"Is he your psychiatrist?" The Officer asked.

"No, but after this, he'll need his own.

Mike laughed. "Dad, you're so funny."

The officer placed Mike and Bruce in the back of the police car and asked another officer to bring Dr. Morgan to the police station. Finally, the officer leaned in and spoke into his shoulder microphone, "Dispatch 5150, 10-19."

Mike and his father had been sitting alone at the table in the police station's interrogation room for an hour, waiting for what would happen next. Passing officers checked on them through the window as they walked by.

44

Their court-appointed lawyer entered the room. "Hello," the woman in a business suit said as she walked through the door. "I'm your attorney. My name is Debbie Alisio."

Mike replied, "Hello. Not to be rude, but I realize that you represent me, and all of this is subject to attorney-client privilege; however, I really can't tell you much. Our doctor, sorry, my doctor, will be here soon."

"OK. I'll wait until he comes."

During the uncomfortable silence, Mike laughed out loud and added, "Shhhhhhhh."

"Is there something funny?" The lawyer asked.

"No. I'm sorry. It's just something my dad said."

"Just said?" The lawyer looked at him with raised eyebrows.

"Never mind."

Twenty minutes later, Dr. Morgan and another man in a suit entered the door. The lawyer stood. "I'm Debbie…"

The man in the suit interrupted her as he presented his FBI credentials and took a seat. "You're the court-appointed attorney, Debbie Alisio. I'm Agent Mancini, and you're excused."

"I'm not leaving unless my client asks me to."

Dr. Morgan looked at Mike and Bruce and took a seat. "It's great to see you again. You know why she can't be here."

"Of course," Bruce said. "Ms. Alisio, you're excused."

"Fine then." She grabbed her bag and walked out the door. "But I'm informing the judge."

Dr. Morgan informed the prisoners that he had just updated the FBI agent about the situation in the lobby moments ago.

The Agent began, "So, gentlemen, you killed a patient today. Can you tell us why?"

Dr. Morgan suggested, "And please let us know who is speaking."

"Mike. I didn't kill him."

"Bruce. Neither did I. You did, against my will."

"Mike. No, you did, and I had no interest in it. We didn't go there to kill him, but we did bring the gun just in case."

"Bruce. You brought the gun. We only bought it because I won, rock, and you had paper. We should have done two out of three."

"Mike. I hate guns. I would never have touched it. You brought it just in case."

The agent said, "Mike, you said, 'just in case.' Just in case of what?"

"Mike. Just in case there were any signs of trouble in the guy, such as instability or other personality issues. Whoever shot him probably did it out of mercy and had a lot of sympathy. Maybe the shooter recognized that man's kind of situation."

"Bruce. He shouldn't have to live spending the rest of his life suffering, and he likely would have chosen to die, but they don't allow you to end your life in mental institutions."

The agent sighed, "I'm going to have to charge you with first-degree murder."

"Mike. Which one of us?"

"Bruce. Me or my son? You can neither determine nor prove that either of us as individuals killed him."

"Mike. Even if you could, the other one is completely innocent. Try sending an innocent man to prison for something he didn't do. Any novice reporter will bust that story wide open."

The agent looked at Dr. Morgan. "Damn, this is messy."

Dr. Morgan replied, "See, I told you. The best thing you can do is a cover story. I know the FBI is good at that, but I'll offer my help to keep the lid on the ASP. I would advise that you contact your superiors immediately. Mention my name."

The agent stood, took out his cell phone, and left the room.

"Dr. Morgan, this is Bruce. We will never have to do this again if they stop these experiments."

"Well, I'm sure all the media outlets captured the results on their cameras. I can confidently say that the public will finally demand that this science stop after today. And I'll be around as always to make sure it does."

Minutes later, the agent walked back into the room. "You're free to go. Just remember that if this ever happens again, someone looking for justice or revenge might take a shot at you. You never know who that might be." He held his stare too long and then started to leave.

"No, I'm sure he directed that toward me!" Mike replied. Their eerie blended laughter was another confirmation that the two souls had joined.

Before he entered the door, Dr. Morgan said, "Agent, if anything like what you just said happens to them, you can expect me and my good friend Margaret Stedman to come after you. I think you may have heard of her. She is known to some as 'the Bulldog.' Ever heard of her? From the LA Report newspaper?"

"Yeah, we know who she is. We know who you are, too," Dr. Mogan said firmly before leaving.

"Now get lost, you two, and stay low for a while. Grow your hair and beard or something so people don't recognize you." Dr. Morgan grinned. "But it is good to see you again."

They stood, shook hands, and began to walk out, saying, "It's good to see you again," Bruce said.

Dr. Morgan sat at his desk, continuing his crusade against the development of what he calls 'soul meddling.' He reviewed the outline of the novel he was writing, ensuring it included his clear ideology, strong opinions, and further warnings about the science. His book detailed the progressing scenario he shared with the Senate subcommittee. Once he finished writing, he published his novel, which many people found genuine and compelling. He titled it "Super Soul, Super Trouble," with the subtitle, "No Trespassing."

"Maybe this is my penance for my part in the catastrophes. Or maybe I needed to be so involved, having seen the development up close, to be qualified to lead the passionate pushback. Who is better than me? Who is more regretful, having not only walked the trail of devastation but also taken the first step and led the way?"

Seventeen Injured People

There are plans and stages within plans. Most people involved in any secret plan should only be aware of the stage they're engaged in and nothing about the entire plan. At most, each link in the chain would know only the end of its involvement, not the one before it or the beginning of the next one. Ironically, this chain is strong because the knowledge of each link is limited. This method is standard when executing a large scheme that requires secrecy and security. Dr. Morgan disliked the plan and was one of the few people who knew the entire details. He also understood the reason for the plan, but he had his own opinion on how it should end.

Seventeen men and women of various ages and races have been heavily sedated and restrained in their beds within a large, secure room located in the basement of the National Center for Science. A tranquilizing drug was secretly mixed into their evening meals at the inpatient facility. Each of these former Advanced Soul Project test patients had a clipboard attached to the foot of their bed. Dr. Carol Brown and Dr. Sydney Morgan conversed in heated tones while nervous orderlies stood silently against a wall. Next to them stood Jim, an armed guard. He was Dr. Brown's informant and preferred to avoid being around the patients. He was assigned to provide security for her and had just enough information about these potentially dangerous test subjects to feel uneasy in their presence.

Dr. Brown's secret government-sponsored ASP had rejected this group of seventeen human experiments after having disappointing results from attempts to have their souls upgraded. The procedures were pitched to the prospective candidates as a "new scientific breakthrough," but the experimentation was more uncertain. At this final rejection stage, these test subjects should proceed to the morgue, just as previous subjects did. Initially, these seventeen victims were scheduled to be secretly euthanized with lethal injections, having never been convicted of a crime. Simply put, they failed to transform into superior individuals.

"I'm totally against this, but you're the famous doctor and author!" Dr. Brown said. "And you threatened the senators into having a conscience!"

"Carol, did funding and deadlines make you rush it through? 'If Joshua had ever been ready for public introduction, clearly today wasn't the day you did it!"

"I just needed more time! I was getting there!" she said, shifting her eyes as her nervous hand rubbed her face.

Dr. Morgan locked his eyes on hers. "He was unstable, but you already made the grandiose announcement. You drugged him up and pushed him on the stage!" He gestured to the seventeen patients. "And look at this carnage! You don't even know what the hell you're doing! You're destroying people's lives!"

Dr. Brown took a step forward. "Just because you oversee them doesn't mean that one misstep won't change everything for you and them!"

"Carol, if something does happen to them or me, I've arranged for all of this to get out to the world, including how ninety people are suffering at 'your' hand!"

"You didn't have the guts to push ahead with the science when you were in charge, Sydney. Now you'll have to watch from the sidelines!"

"It became morally wrong when we realized the soul is too marvelous and complex to understand! You and your team are clumsy and arrogant!"

Dr. Brown stormed out, yelling, "You haven't heard the last from me!"

"I'm watching you! One day, you'll pay for this!" Dr. Morgan yelled to the vacant doorway.

After he composed himself, he signaled the nervous orderlies to start, who pretended to ignore the conversation. They approached the beds, lifted each patient, and placed them onto stretchers. From there, the patients were taken to the guarded loading dock and loaded into various inconspicuous vans. Jim, a US sailor, climbed into the last van.

Several vans departed the hospital at three-minute intervals and took different routes to the seaport. Advancing headlights cut through the darkness, further obscuring the clear objective of dividing the convoy en route to the waiting Coast Guard ship.

When the sleeping patients arrived at the dock, they were taken out of the vans and wheeled into the secured infirmary on the Coast Guard ship, where they would rest through the night.

A seaman offered coffee to Dr. Morgan and his team of medical professionals, experts, and scientists as they sat on the deck. They all ordered coffee, figuring it would be an eight-hour trip to the island. Privately, Dr. Morgan grieved over this mess. Over the years, he had won battles against this kind of experimental science, but the ASP was developed secretly and without his knowledge. Ironically, he was the one who had to clean up the broken pieces of the failed science project that neither he nor anyone else had made or dropped. Now, he must hide the pieces and explain how and why they are broken. They'll have to live in a symbolic trash can in their new island home, which is his greatest challenge in communicating.

The Army Corps of Engineers had already completed its work and departed from the small, uninhabited tropical island. Part of their orders involved clearing rocks and constructing an area on the beach for small rafts to land. They also deployed and anchored special electronic surveillance buoys around the island. Lastly, the engineers built twenty small square concrete structures. Each one contained just a single room with a door and two windows. The engineers didn't know why they had to prepare the island in that manner and were instructed not to ask. Each one held onto whatever opinion from within their team seemed most logical. They all speculated, and none of them was correct. No, the island wasn't intended to serve as a military training site or an early warning radar installation. They prepared the island to be an internment camp for broken people, a secret settlement that carried the stigma and feel of a leper colony.

The 58 acres of Casper Island

In the morning's first light, the Coast Guard ship dropped anchor about a half-mile off the shore. The patients, who were gradually coming out of sedation, were assisted into rubber rafts and taken to the island's beach. A few of them needed to be carried or supported. The wind from the moving rafts and the sound of the motors helped to awaken the patients' dormant senses.

From the rafts on the beach, the patients were gathered and guided through the sand and up the dirt path to sit in a circle of green resin chairs situated in the area between the two rows of twenty unpainted cinder block buildings with fireplaces.

Jim watched with concern as the medical staff carefully walked around the circle, checking each patient's vital signs, whispering questions and comments, and explaining prescriptions. Dr. Morgan volunteered to help serve coffee and snacks to the sleepy and confused group.

Dr. Morgan stood at the edge of the circle as the staff finished, looking around at the patients preparing to hear the unimaginably terrible news.

"Ladies and gentlemen, may I have your attention, please?" He paused as drowsy heads slowly looked up, and sleepy eyes tried to focus on the older man dressed in a regular-looking jacket, not in white scrubs. "My name is Dr. Sydney Morgan. I'm the Director of these people here in the white lab coats. Besides being the leader of this team, I'm also a kind of liaison between you and the government. You were transported here after being disqualified and dismissed from the Advanced Soul Project." He was unaware that his flat tone, bullet-point style of speech, and matter-of-fact approach were the subconscious products of his controlled anger and frustration with the experimental results before him.

"You didn't meet the expectations of the ASP committee, whatever those were." He spread his hands and twisted at the waist to look around. "This is your new home. Each of you will live in one of these buildings, which are humbly furnished with the basics. Buildings eighteen and nineteen already have food, water, and general supplies. Building twenty has a couple of shelves with books, magazines, the tools you'll need for a garden, basic maintenance, and recreational items. You'll get more supplies once a month. I'll go over the details with you tomorrow." He pointed beyond the circle. "There is a crude toilet over there about ten yards that way, and a crude shower area about ten yards over there on the opposite side. I'm sorry, but you must do your best with them. The island has no electricity or plumbing, and won't get any. Near the end of these buildings is a brick fire pit where you can cook and three picnic tables where you can eat. Those are the basic facts of this unfortunate living arrangement. I'm sure you have many questions, so I'll address them one at a time and point to the person with their hand raised.

Adrenaline and confusion began to flow through each of them as the harsh reality invaded their minds. With angry expressions and bewildered looks, the questions demanded answers as hands were raised. Dr. Morgan pointed to the first raised hand.

"Yes?"

"How long will we have to be here?"

"That has not been determined yet, but I plan on settling in and being here for weeks, months, or who knows how long. It's not up to me."

Dr. Morgan pointed at another half-raised hand as the groggy patients quietly objected to the last answer.

A confused woman wrapped in a blanket shook her head as she asked her question. "So, I'm not getting it. What's the purpose of all this?"

"This island is the result of an arrangement I made with the government to keep you alive. They didn't plan on keeping you alive after your procedures, but I intervened and proposed this compromise during the negotiations. My offer was accepted with significant reluctance. But they understood that woven into my offer was an unspoken threat that I would expose them, so they agreed."

"Are you the same Dr. Sydney Morgan who authored those books?"

"Yes, that's me. If you read my books, you should know my clearly stated personal and professional positions against what was done to you."

Dr. Morgan pointed to another raised hand. "You, there."

"Doctor, when can we call our families?"

"You can't, ever."

"What?! Why?!"

With a sigh, Dr. Morgan replied, "Because your families think you're dead."

Angry protest voices escalated from confused mumbling to loud, unintelligible shouts. Standing by the nearest building, Jim stepped forward with his hand resting on his holstered weapon, often staring at them with evident dislike. Like most people, he secretly feared what he didn't understand. Fear and hate, held at a distance, often reveal ignorance.

Dr. Morgan continued with his palms extended toward him.

"Hold on, folks! Try to remain calm and understand! Contacting anyone for any reason was part of the negotiations they wouldn't allow. Listen to me!... They made tragic mistakes with you. They concluded that the changes they made in your souls were mostly for the worse, and they couldn't let you out in public that way. All of you were accidents; vases that cracked in the potter's oven and were rejected. They didn't want the public to know about the embarrassing damage they caused you." Dr. Morgan paused to let that sink in. "Each one of you had a funeral. The caskets were sealed and locked so the mourners wouldn't discover the sandbags inside."

Protesting voices rose again, demanding an explanation. "Wait! Hold on! You must try to understand that you are still alive despite all the bad news! Your lives, this island, and my overseeing it all are what I could take away from the table. I rescued you. You're all alive." He swept his arm from one side of them to the other. "All of you should be dead right now. You were scheduled to die two days ago, but you're still alive." He stabbed his thumb into his chest. "I was the proverbial last-minute phone call from the governor that stayed your executions." Silence and a sense of gratefulness finally started to settle on them. It would seem to any objective listener that the doctor might have overdone it, emphasizing the nearness of their deaths. But he did it to settle them with a sense of 'At least we're still alive' and to foster an attitude of, 'Okay, let's do this and make the best of it.' Each person began their new primitive life with sixteen other people sitting beside them, whom they didn't know.

"This island is called the Community of Advanced Soul Project, or Casp. And I hope you don't mind being nicknamed 'Caspers.'"

Another hand was raised. "Dr. Morgan, my name is Randy, and I read your books." He stood up to look around at the others. "I regretfully took the risk and agreed to participate in the ASP because they told me the technology was a superior and newly tested science. I was supposed to become a superior soldier. Even in this nightmare," he pointed emphatically at Dr. Morgan, "We're fortunate to have this man in charge. He's already demonstrated that he has our backs, and I'm sure he'll continue to have our best interests in mind.

"Thank you, Randy. Now, let's get you all to your private homes. Your names are on the doors labeled with your new addresses, numbers one through seventeen. Take your chairs with you. Look around. Some of you will need help. You'll find a small bed, rugs, and a table inside. Linens, toiletries, and towels are in the dresser, and there's a place to hang your clothes. Place the chairs on your little tables, where you'll find a kerosene lantern and candles. We've stocked clothing and shoes in your respective sizes. There is firewood beside your fireplaces, but you'll need to cut more later. You can begin with some of the dry driftwood along the shore. My team and I will stay overnight on the ship and return in the morning to spend more time with you. We'll bring your breakfast with us. Try to settle in for the night and consider how to best personalize your home. If anyone among you is skilled in crafts, you might consider making decorations and curtains in the future. Each person needs to collect firewood for their house. Lastly, you have noticed the kerosene torches around the area. You'll need to refill them as needed. Help yourselves to the supplies in the storage building – they're all for you. Have the best day and night you possibly can. Try to get some rest tonight." He paused and pointed to a man who still appeared to be heavily drugged. Lastly, Dennis is the gentleman sitting over there. He's unresponsive and requires almost constant assistance. Dennis needs to be fed, changed, and wear diapers like a baby. He can walk slowly. I hope at least one person here has the compassion to attend to him. Just remember, he wasn't this way before the ASP experiments. He went into the procedure as a brilliant veterinarian. Our staff will assist him to his house and put him to bed. See you in the morning.

The Doctor returned to the beach, gently shaking his head. His emotions could finally express themselves through his eyes, and he began to tear up. These emotions also prevailed after he left the other four secret CASPs, having revealed the situation to them.

As the sound of the boat motors faded, the Caspers began their first day alone. Some stayed in their homes, lying on their beds and crying before getting up to numbly open drawers to examine their new clothes and toiletries, most of which they wouldn't have chosen. Others gathered in small groups to introduce themselves, exchanging names and questions. One Casper took a private walk around the island, stopping at the beach to watch the waves, then gazing out over the sea, wondering which direction home was.

Randy, aged 27 years, understood the importance of these strangers finding cohesion and a sense of community as soon as possible. He went to the storage building and searched the shelves, finally discovering coffee cups, tea, and a five-gallon potable water container. Gathering everything, he placed it on one of the picnic tables. Like most people, Randy knew that a fire had a particular effect on the human psyche, so he started a fire in the fire pit and then walked back to his home to retrieve his green resin chair. He shook hands with the first person to approach – a guy in his late thirties.

"Hi. I'm Randy."

"And I'm Charlie. Glad to meet you. Army, huh?"

"Yes,"

"I saw part of your tattoo under your sleeve."

"Oh, that. Yeah. Charlie, could you please bring your chair out here? We all need to get to know each other, and forming a circle might help."

"Sure. No problem. I'll be right back."

As expected, others gradually made their way over with their green chairs to the new central point, forming a circle of Caspers.

Randy smiled. The fire, the circle, and the fresh aroma from the metal coffee pot sitting on the grate had begun the bonding process.

The Caspers spent hours taking turns introducing themselves and sharing brief personal biographies. They came from various backgrounds and occupations. It appears that each of them was selected to participate in the ASP procedure to enhance their occupational skills.

"Who likes to cook?" Randy asked. Several people raised their hands. "Great. Can the four of you get together later and devise a schedule and menus?"

They all agreed. More chores were assigned, as everyone agreed to wash dishes or keep the kerosene lanterns full. Some women suggested that the toilet area needed more privacy and that a proper shower should be in the shower area, so a construction crew was formed. Care for Dennis was discussed, and the Caspers volunteered to take turns providing half-day care.

"Friends, we don't know how long we'll be here, so we need to make the best of it. I hope many friendships will be formed. While we'll form a loving community, each person's privacy must be recognized. Our homes are our private refuge, and we need to respect that. No one should enter another's home unless invited to do so or in an emergency." Heads nodded in agreement.

Natasha raised her hand. "I just really hope we can make this into a loving community. I, for one, will ensure I don't get confrontational."

Sharon smiled and asked, "What should we name our street? Any ideas?"

Smiles formed for the first time as names were offered: 'Oceanside Street,' 'Shoreview Drive,' Palm Avenue.' But 'Unity Lane' was eventually voted the winner. Sharon volunteered to make the sign.

Lee announced, "I live at Seven, Unity Lane in…" Everyone fell silent as the truth that they didn't know the location of the secret island crept back into their minds. He sensed the shift and pushed back against it. "Seven, Unity Lane in downtown Casper City! You can write me at that address or stop by anytime!" Grins spread across the blank faces before gentle laughter replaced the uncomfortable silence.

Joanne added, "The traffic gets thick around the rush hour, but anyone can usually make it to my house in about twenty seconds!" Everyone appreciated the extra levity.

Randy said, "Thank you all for your great attitudes. There will be bad days and little issues, but we're all adults. I intend to become friends with all of you if you have me as your friend." The heads nodded in agreement.

As the sun sank into the sea, the torches were lit along the path to the restrooms and in front of each house. One by one, the Caspers bid good night, took their chairs from the circle, and returned to their small homes to retire for the evening. The warmth of the glowing candlelight spilling through the windows created an impression of Unity Lane being cozy, safe, and settled. However, the façade only masked the sorrow and pain of the restless minds within.

Alone now, Randy remained to watch the fire pit for hours. He sat in his green resin chair, gently stirring the orange coals with the steel poker while he thought. He knew his thoughts were clearer, deeper, and broader than ever before. After gathering and organizing his thoughts and feelings about his current situation, he concluded that he wouldn't stay on the island any longer than necessary.

A scream rang out from one of the small houses. With the aid of the only two remaining lit torches, Randy jumped up and hurried to find the source of the sound. He paused in front of Jon's house, listening to him moan and argue in his sleep as he fought through a nightmare. Randy waited until the struggle ended and the house fell silent again. He hoped that his new friend, Jon, had won that battle. However, Jon's war with his new condition was another matter altogether.

Randy walked a long loop around all twenty buildings in the stillness of the night. Sounds of quiet sobbing drifted from a few homes. After putting out the last torch, he entered his house and lay awake on his bed, tossing and turning for most of the night.

The following morning, Dr. Morgan and his team returned to the island, which resembled a primitive summer camp for youths. Seamen brought large metal pans filled with scrambled eggs, pounds of bacon, seasoned home fries, and thick pancakes from the small rafts. Hot coffee was delivered in two large aluminum pots. Everything was laid out on the picnic tables for the new residents.

The doors of the little houses opened one by one as the sleepy residents emerged with their chairs to eat breakfast. Before heading to the picnic tables, a few lingered outside their doors, glancing around, trying in vain to convince themselves that yesterday wasn't just a bad passing dream. But it was morning, and often, things look better in the morning. A new day was born as the warm sun slowly rose through the palm trees, and the cool ocean breeze respectfully made its presence known. Most of the Caspers agreed that if they had to live this way, a tropical island was the best place to be.

Dr. Morgan helped serve breakfast. Some medical staff observed while others attended to the more severe cases among the Caspers.

After breakfast, Dr. Morgan guided a few of the outcasts around. First, they walked to the supply building, where labeled boxes of food, dishes, pots, pans, cleaning products, books, toiletries, and medical supplies filled the shelves that lined the interiors of buildings eighteen and nineteen. He was assured that the supplies for each month would last until the cargo plane made another delivery on the first of every month.

Building twenty, the tool shed was located thirty feet away on the other side and was stocked with shovels, rakes, seeds, handsaws, buckets, garden stakes, hammers, nails, and ladders. Randy agreed with one of the men from the construction crew that one of the blue plastic drums could somehow be elevated, filled with water, and used for showers.

After hours of talking, showing, and explaining, everyone understood what was where and what they could never have. Dr. Morgan suggested that these strangers try to form a community as soon as possible by assigning chores and responsibilities and establishing meal times, shower times, and other routines.

"All of that was done yesterday afternoon," Randy said.

"Impressive!" Dr. Morgan replied. "Already, you're becoming a community."

Once Dr. Morgan and his team finished everything on their list, it was time for them to leave. He promised to visit regularly and apologized for the basic and crude living situation, then apologized for "the whole damn thing."

Randy walked the doctor to the beach. "Dr. Morgan, we need a few more things."

Dr. Morgan took a small notebook and a pen from his jacket. "Anything you ask for is considered a request and has to be approved. What would you like to ask for?"

"We need some garden hoses, a way to filter seawater, some tarps for bathroom privacy, a showerhead, and a dog."

"A dog?"

"Yeah. A dog is to be everyone's pet. Preferably a German Shepherd puppy. It'll bring some joy and companionship."

"That shouldn't be too hard. I'll see if I can arrange for the other items to be delivered in the next cargo crate, and I'll try to bring you a dog next month when I visit."

"Thank you. I'd appreciate it if you could." Randy only shared the warm and fuzzy reasons with him. However, he understood that once bonded with the Caspers and trained, the dog would serve as an early warning system for any surprise visits.

Almost a year later, on the first of the month, six appointed Caspers watched from a safe distance just inside the island's dense tropical landscape, accompanied by their two bridled horses and a pup named Bear. As the military airplane flew overhead, a large gray wooden cargo crate with airbags on the bottom fell from the back. A massive blue parachute opened to carefully guide the gray crate down to the island's sandy beach. The six people on the beach waved as the airplane departed. Tilting the wings back and forth, the pilot replied, 'I see you, you're welcome, and goodbye.' It's always the same crate, number 5. The Caspers wondered if there were crates numbered 1-4 and ones labeled #6 and above.

The two horses were led to the cargo crate. The parachute was detached, gathered, and thrown into the returning crate thirty yards away. After loading the supplies onto the horses, the team made their way back through the sand and up the dirt trail they had carved long ago through the trees and bushes to transport the cargo crate's contents to the small secret town of twenty square concrete homes.

At the community center, boxes of food, water, magazines, books, clothes, basic toiletries, and medical supplies were unloaded from the horses and sorted on the picnic tables for inventory. Finally, all supplies were placed on shelves in buildings 18 and 20. The hay bales were taken directly to the horse pasture and placed under the large green tarp. The community was always eager to see if the additional items they had requested on the previous month's form were approved and included in the monthly delivery.

After the Caspers left the beach, a massive helicopter hovered over last month's cargo crate, which always arrived an hour after the cargo plane. The crate was partially filled with broken items, worn-out clothing, a bag of used disposable diapers, empty boxes, and unusable refuse that the Caspers had accumulated throughout the month. Also inside were two boxes sealed with red tape labeled "Biohazard," containing used bandages, syringes, empty prescription bottles, and other types of medical waste. The wind from the spinning blades pushed sand away as a large hook at the end of a thick steel cable was guided down onto the metal eye on top of the cargo crate, which was then pulled into the cargo hold. The helicopter flew away. It was a monthly 'leave one and take one' operation. Another routine involved the Coast Guard ship, which occasionally circled the island, except for the mid-month visit when it brought a team of doctors, specialists, and scientists led by retired Dr. Morgan. This process has continued for the past year since these patients were taken to the island.

Eventually, among the seventeen members who were rejected, they came to understand that their skills, special abilities, new knowledge, and heightened intelligence had been discovered through the procedures. These assets included music, various skills, knowledge of technology, physics, engineering, and agriculture. As these new abilities were found and shared with the group, they all agreed to conceal them from the visiting team.

Unfortunately, many Caspers suffered to varying degrees from the adverse effects of the same ASP procedure. Lee sometimes shuts down for hours at a time, and this could happen anywhere. During those moments, two other Caspers would sit at a table, take him to his house, and help him get comfortable. Once, he sat quietly for almost two days.

Nightmares continued to torment Jon. His occasional screams and thrashing at night woke everyone else. Naturally, the others felt sympathy for him and couldn't fathom the terror that haunted his troubled mind. Typically, someone would enter his house quietly to watch over him until his period of terror had passed.

Tyrone experienced a form of bipolar behavior that sometimes manifested in various ways. He also had occasional seizures. Their loving and patient friends understood this, and the presence of Bear sitting nearby benefits all of them. Bear seemed to sense these episodes before they began and remained close.

After wrongfully declaring them dead, in an arrangement with Dr. Morgan, the government placed the Caspers on this island to conceal them, but later decided to study whether these unique individuals would form a community, exhibit and develop any special abilities, or, ideally, have children. The ASP committee secretly ordered one of the sedated women to be inseminated with sperm from another Casper the night before they left the hospital. The child miscarried early in the first trimester. A small grave marker stood behind the woman's house.

Some Caspers felt they lived in an Area 51-like zone and were not far from the comparison. Blinking buoys around the island, routine Coast Guard checks, and their confinement contributed to this sentiment. They suspected the island was under satellite surveillance and had been designated a 'no-fly' zone because they had never seen or heard airplanes. During tranquil moments, however, a faint hum from the sky betrayed a menacing drone watching over the island petri dish.

Other Caspers felt they were in prison, with the formidable sea as the bars and razor wire.

The Caspers had already selected a leader to represent them, named Randy Dickensen. He came from the Army and rarely spoke about it. He was enthusiastic about directing projects and did his best to keep everyone's spirits high. He was also helpful, well-organized, friendly, intelligent, and kind. They chose Randy because he appeared to be one of the most capable and balanced test subjects. The other Caspers wondered if he had any adverse effects from the procedure. He did. At night, when everything was quiet, Randy found it difficult to sleep as his mind was flooded with new thoughts, ideas, voices he had never heard, and images he had never seen, each demanding his attention. Every night, he exercised mental discipline and meditated for an hour before he could sleep. He usually fell asleep and awoke with the same thought—a plan to escape this island. This plan was gradually taking shape. Recently, he began sharing his plans with a few other Caspers.

Sitting on a blanket in the warm sand, Marsha, Olivia, and Bear had just spotted the Coast Guard ship and watched as it moored about half a mile off the shore. They always brought Dennis along because they hoped he would enjoy the company of the different species of birds that gathered around him while he sat and stared at nothing. The birds flew to him and no one else, even though he had never fed them. There was something about Dennis that the birds liked and something Bear sensed. Since his ASP procedure, Dennis could be described as a person in a coma who could only walk slowly, and his friends fed him mashed food. He didn't feel the indignity of being unable to change his diapers. Changing him was simply something the others were used to doing. Dennis seemed to have an impact on other animals as well. Whenever he walked by the small horse pasture, even though he never gave them treats or realized the horses were there, they whinnied and ran to the fence while Dennis kept shuffling by, assisted by whoever was taking him for the walk. The goats and chickens reacted the same way.

By now, the Caspers had become accustomed to witnessing the subtle powers and unique nuances displayed by each soul. These changes aimed to customize and enhance their souls with the best features from others. Just as taking pieces from one puzzle and expecting them to fit into another won't yield the beautiful mountain scenery promised on the box, the ASP experimental procedures involving removing and adding portions of one soul to another did not produce superior human beings. While new science and discoveries often lead to advancements, they can also result in regrets. When that happens, someone must pay the price, typically the person lying on the operating table. This time, it was the Caspers who were paying dearly.

Marsha walked back between the two rows of concrete houses to the new community center at the end to tell Randy that the Coast Guard ship had been sighted. Randy and the others appreciated Dr. Morgan, the leader of the science team, not only for his opposition to soul manipulation but mainly for his warmth and compassion. Randy rang the bell four times—the signal that announced the monthly visit. Bear had learned what the four rings meant; he barked and ran to the beach to watch.

Most of the Caspers had gathered on the sandy beach to welcome the arriving team. They watched as the large rubber motorboat filled with people approached. Some island residents ambled down to the shore with help from the other Caspers. They, along with the man they sometimes had to carry, dealt with issues related to the ASP Dr. Morgan, who had figuratively elbowed his way into the project after the public assassination of Joshua Sims, insisted that all their lives be spared, even those with serious issues. The government had already learned that there were two people they didn't want to cross again. Dr. Sydney Morgan was one, and Margaret Stedman, the editor of the LA Report, was the other, especially when they teamed up. It was a bittersweet situation for Dr. Morgan. He saved their lives, but this prison island was the price they paid. He decided that sometimes you must take what you can get and make the best of it.

There were mixed feelings among the island residents about these monthly visits. It was always good for the Caspers to see the regular team, except for Jim, the armed guard, who insisted on being unfriendly. He had to follow Dr. Morgan's directions, but he was the only one who disrespected him by calling him 'doc.' Bear didn't like him, and the feeling was mutual. The Caspers had a nickname for him: Igor. They agreed that it was a fitting name for being the assistant of the mad scientist, Dr. Brown.

The Caspers enjoyed receiving the 'extra' things Dr. Morgan brought. However, the visits also served as a reminder of 'where' the residents were and, more soberly, 'what' they were. Furthermore, although the visits were friendly and light, most of the reasons for these visits were that everyone had to undergo monthly inspections and evaluations. Part of the inspections involved determining what abilities had developed after the ASP procedures and whether any changes resulted from them. They underwent extensive interviews. The Caspers acted coy and shared little more than minor complaints about sleeplessness or aches. They were a diverse yet close-knit family with different skills and talents, but what they discussed and displayed was confined to themselves and ultimately shared with no one else except Dr. Morgan.

Bear walked into the water and barked a greeting. The others helped each team member as they exited the rubber rafts with their gear. Dr. Morgan, who always looked forward to these visits, waved and smiled at the group gathered before him. Randy approached to meet him with a welcoming handshake after Dr. Morgan gave Bear the treat he always brought.

"Welcome, Dr. Morgan. It's always great to see you!"

Thank you, Randy. I always look forward to seeing all of you. It's the highlight of every month. My wife says she can tell how I act when the middle of the month is near. However, her analogy of a little child on Christmas morning might be a bit of a stretch.

We've prepared coffee, tea, and treats for everyone at the community center. But first, please come with me.

Randy always noticed small amounts of mud on the visitors' shoes and continued to take note of it. The mud didn't come from their island. In his mind, he filed the clue with the number 5 on the cargo crate, alongside the clues regarding the origin and destination of the cargo plane, helicopter, and ship. He hoped that every piece of information, even the seemingly subtlest, could eventually prove helpful in forming a plan to escape.

The Caspers led the long line up the trail, through the center of the two rows of houses, to the newly constructed large bamboo pavilion community center at the far end. The thatched-roof rectangular pavilion had been built since Dr. Morgan's team last visited.

"Wow! This is a lovely pavilion! Nice sturdy tables and wicker furniture, too!" Dr. Morgan said, casually standing with his hands in his pockets. As he looked around at the woven bamboo strips on the half-walls and glanced up at the thick bamboo rafters, he added, "Now I see why you requested the hand tools and hardware. And every house has a new awning and fresh paint!"

The Caspers could choose the color for their homes from a short list of four flat, dark earth tones. Randy, known only to a few, had ordered more tools and hardware than needed for these projects, while Charlie was very particular about the color of paint he ordered for his house.

As the two leaders were served coffee at the table closest to the entrance of the community center, most of Dr. Morgan's team had gathered at the opposite end of the building, setting up their medical equipment to begin the examinations. As always, each Casper's name was called before they were carefully examined and put through multiple tests behind a small portable privacy screen. From there, they proceeded to the next station, where mental health professionals interviewed them. Two visitors in lab coats slowly walked around the small town, observing, recording videos, and taking notes on a clipboard.

"So, Randy, how are things going?" Dr. Morgan asked.

"We've had a few minor issues, but nothing that couldn't be resolved."

"Like what?"

One of us was secretly hoarding food at home. Some others became unhappy with their responsibilities, but all of that has been worked out. We've cleared and planted an area for a large vegetable garden and done much work there. We also made our compost and improved our homes. Finally, we wove palm leaf curtains for everyone's windows. We've just cleared another spot for an orchard for banana trees and other tropical plants that would thrive here. We chose the location because some of the largest bamboo was growing there, which we used to build the pavilion. Now, we have mango trees, papaya trees, grapes, and berry bushes."

"You've all been very busy. After having the two horses approved, most anything else shouldn't seem too difficult. I'll see what I can do, but it'll be a while before the trees mature. Eventually, though, you'll enjoy fresh fruit."

Randy smiled. "The trees will grow quicker than you would expect. You've never watched Natasha sing."

Dr. Morgan squinted his eyes. "What do you mean by that?"

"Dr. Morgan, if I explained it to you, you might not believe it, so we'll show you. Give me a minute."

Randy jogged along the path to invite Natasha to join them for a walk to the expansive garden that some of the Caspers had carved out from the palm trees and bushes.

"Hello, Natasha."

"Hi, Dr. Morgan, Natasha smiled."

As Natasha slowly walked into the garden, rows of color-ripening vegetables and lush plants now flourished in the rich, dark soil. She sang a gentle, melodic tune that seemed to float in the air. The garden quietly hummed in response. She spread her hands and brushed her fingers gently against the leaves of the squash plants that leaned toward her as she walked between the rows. The green tops of the carrots also seemed to bend toward her as she approached, and the raspberry bushes shivered in delight as she passed by. It was as if she were a gracious queen, and the plants were her adoring subjects, eager to reach out and touch her as she leisurely passed.

"That's amazing. It can only be because of Natasha's level of life energy," Dr. Morgan said.

"Maybe she emits a special frequency from her life energy," Randy suggested. "Notice that even the trees and plants around the garden are larger and healthier than the others. Our garden grows very quickly, and the plants live a long time. We get multiple harvests in a single season because of her. The only unfortunate part is that the weeds grow quickly, too."

"Randy, do yourself a favor. Please don't tell anyone on my team about this. It'll just give them another reason to want to test you folks and test you more. In this situation, I'll change the old saying from "Less is more" to "Less is better." The less you tell them, the better off you'll be."

"Dr. Morgan, that's already an established motto with us."

As they stood overlooking the garden, Dr. Morgan said, "Again, I apologize for the lack of convenience. The government is very cautious when granting certain things. Due to the unknown levels of intelligence and abilities in this community, they're afraid of what can be done with even 'basic' technology."

"So, will kerosene torches for light and fireplaces for heat, community outhouses, shrewd showers, and printed entertainment still have to do?"

"At least, for now, Randy. But we've brought you more things today that will take you up a notch and are guaranteed to boost morale. How about we continue our tour?"

"Sure. I'll be glad to show you around more, Natasha said. "Guys, I should return to the pavilion."

"Thank you, Natasha. We'll be there in a few minutes," Dr. Morgan replied.

Randy led Dr. Morgan from the thriving vegetable garden to explain the simple but efficient bamboo irrigation system.

"It's a series of split bamboo channels that start at the windmill and end at those two suspended water barrels. On a breezy day, the handmade windmill drives the seawater through a series of halved coconut shell water wheels and the desalination filter. Then, the freshwater ends up in the elevated blue plastic drums. All of this is thanks to Charlie's engineering skills. He constructed an elaborate yet straightforward system using everyday items, such as pulleys and ropes. When there's no wind, someone can sit on that contraption and provide pedal power."

"Basic, yet it works," Dr. Morgan noted.

At the compost station at the edge of the garden, Randy stuck his hand in the pile and extracted a rich, dark mixture of soil.

"Dr. Morgan, canned vegetables from the monthly shipment are fine, but there's nothing like a fresh home-grown organic salad." He slowly tipped his hand, letting the dirt fall back onto the pile. "It's the same fresh food goal with seafood, so we made fish traps and nets. We plan to create a fish farm once we drive down the posts and attach the nets. Sebastian is leading the effort there."

"Very nice, Randy. I can't imagine how many people would love to have a life like this: living off the grid, simple, healthy, and away from what's becoming close to an uncivilized civilization. Not to mention the close-knit family atmosphere here."

"True. We have grown to love and appreciate each other. But you need to tell anyone interested and ready to fill out the application that once the guests arrive, they can never leave and never contact their families again."

Dr. Morgan nodded and sighed, his face showing compassion. "Yeah. I know, Randy. I know, and I think about it all the time."

"Ready for that second cup of coffee, Dr. Morgan?"

"Sure."

Returning to the community center, they discovered that most Caspers had been examined and tested inside the portable, white-curtained structures.

As they sipped their coffee, Dr. Morgan asked the guard, "Jim, would you please ask the crew to bring up the extra supplies?"

"Of course, Doc." He spoke into his radio to the crew waiting on the beach, who had already loaded and stacked the supplies at the tree line.

"Randy, I managed to get approval on a few special things. If you can believe it, some items were donated by one of the more compassionate Senators overseeing the ASP. Our crew is bringing them up. I hope the community is pleased."

Randy was a bit surprised that Dr. Morgan mentioned a senator. Until now, he hadn't realized specific high-ranking politicians were so directly involved. He wondered if it was intentional or a Freudian slip.

Minutes later, the first crew emerged from the trail, carrying boxes. They placed them on a table for everyone to watch. Dr. Morgan stood up, opened the first box, and pulled out a guitar.

"This is for Theresa." He looked around for her while holding the guitar. "Theresa, where are you? I believe you're the one who asked for this."

She walked over briskly with a huge smile. "Oh, thank you! I've never played one, but my grandmother was a classical guitarist, and I feel her music in me. And somehow, I already know chords, so this should be easy! Now, all we need is a piano!" she laughed.

"Well, what a coincidence because here comes one now!" Dr. Morgan said as eight men awkwardly carried a heavy crate toward them. The wooden crate was unstrapped, the door swung open, and an upright piano was pulled out.

"A piano?! Really?!" Theresa's eyes grew wide.

"Yes," Dr. Morgan replied with a smile. "It's an upright model, but there's also a tuner. I imagine it'll have to be tuned frequently in this moist air. Have I mentioned that in these other boxes are a violin and music books? We threw in a harmonica just in case. Imagine the concerts you and the others can put on! Also in these boxes are flashlights and a battery-operated radio, all of which come with plenty of extra batteries. I don't know how many channels you can get, but it'll be somewhat of a connection to the world."

69

"Set the piano right here near this side wall, please," Randy instructed the men. "And leave the empty crate if you can. We could use the wood for another compost bin."

Silently, Randy noted the metal hinges. They are what he wants the most. The wood won't be used for another compost bin.

After the commotion had settled somewhat, Dr. Morgan announced, "And last but not least."

The men from the beach walked up the trail with two dozen Rhode Island Red chickens in crates for eggs and a rooster. They also brought rolls of chicken wire, staples, and a wire cutter.

"The wire and tools are in case you don't want to free-range them. Lastly, two milking goats." The Caspers all clapped together. After the applause died down, Dr. Morgan looked at them with a serious expression. "I know this situation isn't good, but I want all of you to know I'm doing everything possible to improve it." Everyone expressed their appreciation for his efforts.

After the last Casper, Randy was examined, and proper notes were taken. It was time for Dr. Morgan's team to return to the Coast Guard ship. Randy and a few others escorted the team back to their boats. Dr. Morgan pulled Randy aside.

Randy, don't forget I'm working my angles for you and the others. But it all leads back to the politicians, and I'm a doctor.

"Dr. Morgan, I never forget… anything. I remember everything, good and bad. And I don't get confused; I lack information. Please see what you can do to get us off this island. We want to go home."

"I've tried many times through the proper channels and spoken with the senators on the secret committee, but they won't allow it because they and Carol Brown have a lot at stake."

He leaned toward Randy, pretending to brush something off his shoulder. "If you're going to get off this island, you'll have to figure out a way and tell me nothing about it. And I'm forbidden to write anything publicly about the Caspers. I'm sorry." Dr. Morgan casually stepped back. "Do you have your list of requests for my next visit?"

Randy took out the folded form from his shirt pocket. "Yes. Here you go."

Dr. Morgan put on his glasses, unfolded the form, and read it. "Randy, as a way of helping convince them to approve your request for solar panels, finally, let's use the strategy of that old saying, 'If you want a dog, ask for a horse.' Do this. Ask for a large generator, but tell them you'll settle for solar panels with batteries. Please write that you want to install them for the houses' lights, hot plates, and coffee-makers. I'll suggest to them that you need electricity for a radio so that we can talk at any time in case of emergencies. But let me caution you. If you get the electricity, they might want to install observation cameras. So, think about it. Consider the trade. Randy, I know how they feel. At the same time, I must be frank with you. We may be pushing against what is already a politically fragile and vulnerable line. There are still some in the government who want to end this community. Try to see it from their side. There's a lot of effort on their part to justify keeping this island going. It's costly; they have to hide it in the budget, they're growing weary of maintaining the secrecy, and they're chronically nervous about the risks."

"What is the risk of revealing the ASP's failures or their lies?

"Both." Dr. Morgan stared at Randy for a few seconds in silence to make the implication of danger clear again. "But I push back, reminding them of the scientific value and potential of the Caspers. I suggest that the 'specimens' here can never be replicated and, therefore, should be preserved like we have preserved samples of eradicated viruses. I have to use such comparisons and jargon to keep them at bay. One last thing: just as that possibility exists, there's more unsettling news. The senators want to get something in return for their investment. Finally, I was asked to inform you that Dr. Brown intends to bring the individuals here back for further testing now that the situation has settled down—one of you at a time, starting next month, with Dennis as the first.

Randy whispered with alarm, "Dennis?! He came out of the procedure in worse shape than anyone else! Those bastards. Will they bring him back? Will they bring 'any' of us back? Will we come back the same way we left?"

"Randy, I don't know the answers to any of those questions."

71

"Doctor, they have just pushed us into a corner. I can't let them pick us off one at a time. That won't happen on my watch. None of us will be taken from this island alone. It's all or none."

Dr. Morgan whispered back, "Do what you have to do. Again, don't tell me your intentions. However, carefully request what you need to get out of your corner on the form. Focus on the crates, Randy. Focus on the crates."

Suddenly, soft but beautiful music from the piano, violin, and guitar playing at the community center caused them both to turn and look. The gentle music reminded them of the real people here, talented individuals they had grown to love. Initially, the music made Dr. Morgan feel very relaxed. A few quiet moments later, he felt as if he had been slightly sedated and struggled to keep his eyes open. He managed to lift his arm and put it on Randy's shoulder to steady himself.

"Wow," he mumbled. "What is this? I feel like I've been drugged."

"I'm sorry, Dr. Morgan. I can feel it, too. The music also makes me feel a little spacey. It must be that life energy has found another expression through whoever is playing."

That evening, the residents gathered at the community center for supper and settled around the tables as usual. After the meal, they lit the torches around the pavilion and cleared the tables to enjoy playing instruments and singing old favorites. The group talked excitedly about how nice it would be to have fresh eggs, goat milk, and cheese. Flashlights and batteries were distributed to each person.

Lily listened to the radio but mostly found foreign language stations and static. She enjoyed translating every primary language for the group, but they all soon grew tired of it. Playfully, she gently shook the radio, trying to find some good music. Then she heard a rattle and exclaimed, "Hey! This thing has a loose part!" She laughed. "It must be the music component."

"Let me see that, Lily," Landon suggested. "Maybe something came loose."

With the help of his new flashlight, he removed the tiny screws. When he opened the back, a small electronic device fell onto the table. While holding it in the palm of his hand and inspecting it with his flashlight, he noticed the dried glue on the back, suggesting that it had once been mounted inside but had fallen off. It was clear that the device was not part of the original product.

"Can you fix it?" Lily asked.

Landon looked at her and placed his index finger before his pursed lips. "Nah, it's just an extra piece of something you don't need. That's why these things cost so much. I'll just put it back inside and try to figure it out later." He pretended to do so. "There, I'll take it home for now." He closed his hand tightly around the small electronic piece, walked over to Randy, and stood close to him. "It's an electronic listening device. A bug. It can be remotely turned off and on."

Randy was troubled by the expression on his face. "Take it to your house and control it. We might be able to use it to our advantage. Come right back. I have some things I need to say to the group."

A few minutes later, Randy stood up from his seat. "I'd like to have everyone's attention, please." Everyone found a seat and grew quiet.

"We're so thankful for the supplies and extra gifts from Dr. Morgan's efforts. He's a good man who has made our exile a little better. But the fact is, we are still here and likely will always be until the last one of us dies or they take us back." The faces turned solemn. "Friends, this island isn't a settlement or a reservation. We live in secret exile. It's punishment for mistakes that we didn't make. It seems to me that some of us are becoming too accustomed to being here and have grown too comfortable. The government could bring in a department store with free merchandise, a spa, an open bar, and a fitness club, but it wouldn't change the fact that we live in captivity. I don't know about you, but no amount of comfort and convenience will change that for me. My freedom is much more valuable than anything they could fit on this island." A few heads nodded. "Before he left, Dr. Morgan told me if we ever got electricity, the government would install what he called 'observation cameras' so they could watch us. They'll sit in some office in Washington with their feet up on their desks and study us on monitors as we walk to the outhouse and sing at the piano. They might even listen to our intimate discussions and discover our unique abilities. Hell, they might even put video cameras inside our homes."

Heads shook as some folks objected with 'No!' while others shouted, 'Never!'

"And if you need evidence, that little piece that Landon found rattling inside the radio is a bug. An electronic listening device. The government wants to see us and listen to us." Gasps came from the group as they looked at each other in surprise. "I'm certain it was placed there without Dr. Morgan's knowledge, but the government intends to eavesdrop on us as part of their study. Friends, as things stand, we'll never see our homes and loved ones again. Now, for the worst news. Beginning next month, they'll take us back one at a time to study, test, and probably subject us to more procedures. One would think those scientists would have a sense of dread by now, given what they've done to us. But no. They want to do more. And we don't know if we'll ever be returned or if we'll be the same people we were when we're brought back. Next month, they intend to start by taking Dennis."

The group turned with compassion to look at the man sitting in his chair, being fed, and blankly staring at nothing, slowly chewing his mashed dinner in silence because something had gone wrong during the procedure to implant parts of someone else's soul code into him. Dennis didn't respond to the announcement because he couldn't. Besides walking slowly, he could open his mouth to be spoon-fed by Joanne, who fed him like a baby. She used the spoon to collect the mash that dribbled down his mouth as he sat there in his adult diaper. His oversized bib protected his shirt from any food that fell.

"I know exactly how this sits with me and how it sits with you. We don't like it. And I have a plan to do something about it. None of you has to join me in my plan, and I'll love you just the same. Others here might want their freedom back enough to join me." The intensity of his voice rose with each new sentence. "I intend to go get a damn computer and some solar panels myself. I intend to build a satellite dish and hack into some systems. I intend to tell the world what we are, where we are, and why!" He paused, lowering his voice as his eyes darted around the group to each staring face. "And at the end of the day, I intend to go home and take all of you with me… every one of you."

Every Casper who could stand on their feet did so and clapped. Many walked over to Randy, patted him on the back, and gave him hugs. They all verbally committed to his ultimate goal of going home and offered to help in any way they could.

The island's residents had thirty days before Dr. Morgan and his team's next visit, and just two weeks earlier, Randy attempted his escape plan.

As the final stage of the plan approached, a small group of Caspers gathered in the pavilion. "Ok. I will need a flashlight, batteries, water bottles, food, a box cutter, two different screwdrivers, and maybe that small pry bar," Randy said. "Charlie, how are you doing with the secret compartment?"

"It's tiny. We finished it this morning. As a precaution, when building it, we hid the materials inside the garbage as we walked back and forth. You never know what those satellites can see. We used boards from the piano crate to construct it, and used the hinges for the door. It'll hold you fine. Thankfully, the doorway of the big cargo crate doesn't extend to the top, so your space can't be seen looking straight in. But Randy, the compartment is tight. You won't have much room to maneuver once we get you in it. There's just enough space to move your arms to take an occasional drink and pee into the bottle. Just don't get the order mixed up. If you forget everything else, don't forget to drink the water first, then you pee into the bottle." Everyone laughed. They always appreciated moments of humor that brought levity.

Charlie added another feature. "On the board, there is a knot that he can remove to see into the crate."

"Good idea," Randy replied. "There's no way to tell how long I'll be in there."

"It's risky, Randy," Landon offered.

"That's the way it must be. Eventually, the compartment will be discovered, probably when the cargo crate is refilled. But I hope to be long gone by then," Randy replied.

Charlie said, "Someone might think they've just added a compartment for long, narrow items like shovels, small boxes, and such, so it might not even get reported. At your suggestion, we painted the outside of the space with some leftover flat gray paint we used to paint my house. And do you know it's nearly the same color as the cargo crate?!"

Landon smiled. "Can you believe that? What are the odds of that happening?"

Randy looked at him, winked, and said, "What a coincidence. It was as if someone had planned all those things." They all chuckled.

"One more thing...," Randy said. "I need to be able to adapt to different scenarios. I might not have a choice. So, in case I can't return as planned, I'll still try to ship the items back here on the next delivery. If I'm not in that crate when it's brought back, or if I don't make it back at all, the plan still goes on. Does everyone understand that?"

"Yeah," they all answered with regretful looks.

"Hopefully, I can get my hands on a couple of radios. Who do we have here that can set up solar panels and a satellite dish?"

Olivia volunteered with a smile. "I can do that, but it will be easier with some directions. In any case, I'll get it done. At least some good things were given to me in the ASP. I never graduated from college, but now I know most of what an electrical engineer knows!" She threw her hands up into the air. "Tada! Who woulda thunk it?"

Lastly, Randy looked at each one of them. "I want to emphasize that if I don't return in two weeks, continue without me. Work together to get that satellite up and make it happen!" Dropping the tip of his finger on the table, he emphasized the mandate. "All of you, get off this damn island and go home with or without me." The other people at the table dropped their eyes down and nodded.

The Escape from Casper Island

Half a dozen Caspers, Bear, and two horses waited at the top of the beach for the cargo plane, two weeks after Dr. Morgan's team had left. The aircraft followed its routine by rolling the massive gray cargo crate off the back as it passed over the beach. The large gray parachute opened, and the gray crate gently settled on the sand with a soft bounce. The Caspers waved 'thank you,' and the plane waved back 'You're welcome' as it flew away. As usual, the Caspers opened the crate and packed the horses before taking them up the trail back to the community center to inventory and store everything.

The cargo crate from the previous month's drop had junk and refuse and was ready to be returned. It had sat on the beach since the last airdrop. The only difference in this monthly routine was that this time, the approaching helicopter would take the cargo crate back with a very determined stowaway hidden inside who knew it would take a combination of skill, luck, knowledge, and quick thinking to make his mission successful.

When the cargo plane disappeared, Randy dashed down from the trees, yanked the door open, and climbed into the cargo crate before the helicopter arrived. Charlie and Landon helped him into the small compartment above the door, ensuring he was settled. They left, pulling the crate's door shut behind them. Randy lay in the mostly dark secret compartment with his small bag under his head, listening to the sound of the approaching helicopter. The loud thrum of the rotors overhead made him envision the massive hook descending in his mind. Moments later, a sharp metal 'clang' confirmed that the hook had latched onto the large metal loop on top. He felt the crate shift as it was hoisted off the sand. Soon after, he sensed a slight swinging motion until the crate was brought into the cargo hold. Once the bottom door was closed, Randy felt the crate settle onto the floor. It became quiet enough for him to hear muffled voices.

"Sergeant, make sure you check through the junk in there."

"Yes, Sir. Right away."

Randy heard the crate's door open and removed the knot. The soldier stepped forward and entered, a flashlight attached to his weapon. He directed the beam of light back and forth as shadows leaned away to hide from the glow. The inside of the crate smelled like dirty diapers because the bag was purposely left partially unsealed. With the end of his weapon, he pushed aside the parachute and gently kicked the boxes of stained clothes and bags of recyclables. A broken shovel leaned against the corner. He couldn't help but notice the partially opened red-taped box labeled BIOHAZARD next to the word CAUTION. The bloody gauze hanging out from the top next to a syringe created the intended effects of disgust and distraction. The other 'Biohazard' box, located behind the first, was still sealed with the same warning tape. The soldier made a disgusted face and decided to leave them both alone. He turned to exit, quickly shutting the door against the putrid smell.

"Clear!"

The sounds of footsteps and the door closing indicated that Randy would at least make it to the military base. In the worst case, he could be discovered and arrested. If that happens, the arrest will be hushed, and he will likely be taken immediately to a secret jail where no one will know until the other Caspers inform Dr. Morgan about his next visit. Furthermore, if the plan fails at this early stage, the entire idea of escape would be over, and there would be no satellite to inform the world of their dilemma.

Randy did his best to estimate the helicopter's speed and recorded the time he took off. When the crate arrives at the base, he'll check his watch again and later try to find a map or use a public library computer to see which island became their prison. He needed to gather the required items in two weeks and return to the island before Dr. Morgan's team visited. He planned to hide in the next cargo crate heading back to the island, but it would be a very long two weeks.

Feeling the helicopter slow down within the tight compartment and stopping to hover, Randy became tense. A hydraulic motor somewhere in the cargo hold turned on. He could tell that his crate was being lifted off the floor. He heard the floor below him open, and the crate was lowered to the ground. Even though he knew the crate had airbags to cushion it upon contact with the ground, he braced himself before it softly bounced and rocked slightly on impact. A metallic 'bang' above the crate suggested the hook had been disengaged before the helicopter flew off. According to his watch, the trip took just under two hours at the helicopter's cruising speed. He knew plenty of time remained before dark, indicated by the tiny beam of light that came through the single small hole drilled for him back on the beach. He also accepted that he would have to continue lying there in that tight space until then and listen for anything that might help him understand where he was. He drank water and waited, grinning as he remembered Charlie's joke about the water bottle.

It was finally dark, and the night was very quiet. Randy pushed the hinged door up and held it open long enough to stretch his cramped legs before lowering himself; he hung his legs out for a few moments, twisted around, held onto the bottom edge of the compartment, and dropped to the floor, carefully landing quietly on his toes. He stood there briefly to stretch his back muscles and check his watch. To diffuse the light from his flashlight, he covered the lens with the palm of his hand and turned it on. After opening the sealed biohazard box, he removed the tools and shoved them into his pockets. He set the small crowbar aside for now. After Charlie modified the crate's door, it wasn't too difficult to open it from the inside. Randy turned off the flashlight, placed the end of a screwdriver under the lever on the door, and carefully raised it. With the tips of his fingers, he gently pushed against the door, opening it about an inch. Distant lights from the main gate allowed him to exit the crate unnoticed. He found himself in a large chain-linked, razor-wired storage yard filled with several other identical crates, random equipment, and multiple vehicles. He noticed a camera mounted high on the wall, facing him. If he were discovered, it would require skill and luck to avoid being caught, resulting in a disaster.

Randy cautiously sneaked outside the building, wearing black pants and a shirt, and kept a constant glance toward the structure. Discovering that the other crates were labeled 1, 2, 3, 4, and 5, he now believed there were different groups of Caspers. Inside the other crates, the contents were similar to his, right down to the Biohazard boxes. He learned that there were two cargo crates with the same number for each Casper location. At that moment, Randy realized his mission would affect many more people like him. There were other victims trapped somewhere far from their homes and families, held against their will due to faulty science or mistakes made by the technicians during the Advanced Soul Project procedures. Perhaps it was a knob turned too far or the voltage in some laboratory gadget that was slightly off. More likely, the mishaps stemmed from a general disregard for human life.

Even though it was a military facility, Randy concluded it was not very secure. He decided it was little more than a lightly guarded military surplus and storage site.

When the door was opened a crack at the back of the building, Randy saw a soldier sitting at the desk, reading over a report inside the office. At that moment, he's unaware of the video monitor above him that showed and recorded Randy's ghostly image appearing and disappearing in the dim equipment yard. At least for now, luck was on Randy's side. Crouching as low as he could, Randy worked his way toward what he believed to be the huge storage building. He was thankful there were so many vehicles, crates, and equipment in the yard to dash to and hide between.

He arrived at the back of the building, looking, walking, and crouching. He ducked behind a bush as a soldier suddenly exited the back door of the building. The guard stood there to smoke his cigarette under the light above the door, casually blowing smoke into the air. Randy timed the smoke break and waited for the soldier to finish. The soldier dropped his cigarette butt on the ground and then went back inside, closing the door behind him. Straining to hear the sound of a lock secured, Randy heard nothing now. As he waited, he thought about his Casper family back on the island to ease his tension. The memories and the bonds strengthened his resolve to succeed. 'Here it goes!' he thought as he crouched over to the door before the guard returned to his desk. Randy knew he might have been seen and recorded by the cameras, but that wouldn't be revealed until the recording was ever checked. If the guard discovered him, he expected to be ready for a fight when he stepped through the door. Or, in the worst case, shot. He opened the door slightly and saw that it led directly into the dark warehouse. About thirty feet to his left, a door leading to an enclosed office area with the lights on was closing. He could see the soldier through the window as he sat at a desk with his back to the window. The guard was listening to music on the radio. Randy hoped that the soldier's audio, visual, and mental senses were stimulated enough not to notice any quiet sounds or movements that he might make in the warehouse.

Further, he realized that the glass window between the lighted office and the dark storage area would act like a mirror inside the office. He slipped through the door and turned toward the vast room filled with stacked palletized boxes on the floor and tall storage shelves against the walls. Randy continued to hope that what he needed was in there as he searched in the faint light from the office. Dimming the light from his flashlight and keeping a watchful eye on the office window, he memorized the stock numbers of the crates that weren't labeled with their contents. He smiled when he saw five sectioned-off areas against the wall. Each section was labeled '1-5'. The varying numbers of open boxes in each section suggested that the orders were still being assembled.

The soldier casually stood up, took his cigarettes and lighter off the desk, and then walked out the office door and the back door. Randy watched him from behind a stack of boxes until the outside door closed. After peering at his watch, he walked quickly and quietly to the office door and went inside. After hurriedly rifling through the papers on the desk in search of an inventory sheet that matched the stock numbers with the item descriptions, he found nothing. However, his eyes were drawn to the corkboard where the inventory sheets were tacked. His mind formed a mental picture of each sheet as he stared at it for ten seconds. After glancing at his watch, he sneaked back through the office door and toward the dark side of the warehouse. Just as he passed the outside door, it began to open. Randy spun to the side and froze against the wall under the red light from the exit sign above, waiting for the soldier to enter. Clenching his fists, Randy was ready to fight in case the guard discovered him, but he was quickly relieved when the soldier walked back to the office. Randy quietly and promptly returned to the storage area, walking close to the wall so the guard wouldn't see him. The soldier's heavy walk masked the sound of his footsteps, and music drifted through the open office door.

Searching for what he needed, Randy stayed there among the boxes and crates for hours. Due to the guard's frequent naps, cigarette breaks, bathroom visits, and his attention to his computer game, Randy discovered foldable solar panels, a small satellite dish, a laptop, two small batteries, the schematics, the electronic equipment needed to make it all work, and two long-distance radios. He packed them in a box, sealed them, and put the box on the stack with the other boxes in section 5. It took him a while to find some BDUs that fit over his clothes and a beret that fit his head. However, locating an Officer's proper rank and insignias took even longer.

After waiting for the guard's next bathroom break, Randy slipped out the door, taking his tools, the radios, and the uniform back to cargo crate 5. After sneaking around the lot while trying to keep out of the camera's sight, Randy located and prepared the wires in a government car he selected to use for his escape. He placed his tools, water bottle, and the radios on the car's floor. Returning to the cargo crate, he decorated the BDU shirt by sewing on patches with a needle and thread and waited for the guard to be replaced on schedule.

Before daylight arrived, the large chain-link gate slid open for the car outside, waiting to enter. The replacement soldier for the day shift drove into the yard, parked his car, and walked into the building. After about fifteen minutes, the night guard stepped out, got into his car, and left through the same gate. Randy, watching from behind the cargo crates, deduced that the gate would open by itself from the inside due to the outline of the metal sensor in the asphalt. The next stage of his plan had to work perfectly, and he wanted to leave before any other warehouse workers arrived.

The warehouse's back door opened abruptly as 'Lieutenant' Randy Dickensen entered. He headed directly to the office, carrying a clipboard and a small bag over his shoulder to conceal the absence of a name tag. The new guard, surprised, heard the door open and spun around in his chair. He jumped to his feet and stood at attention as Randy entered the office.

"As you were."

The Corporal asked, "Sir, how did you get in without me opening the gate?"

Randy's demeanor was agitated, and his voice was fast and impatient. "Number one: I ask the questions, and you answer them. That's the way it usually works. Is that clear, Corporal?"

"Very clear, Sir."

"Corporal, we call these 'surprise inspections' for a reason, emphasizing the word 'surprise.' I've been here all night sitting in my damn car, watching to see how this facility is managed and operates. My job is to observe how the property of the United States government is secured and guarded, and who might have dozed off while on duty. Do I need to remind you of your duties?"

"No, Sir."

"Let me see last night's watchman's log. And get me some black coffee, pronto."

"Yes, Sir."

He handed Randy the clipboard from the desk and poured a cup of coffee as Randy read the log. "There's a lot of bullshit here." He looked up at the Corporal. "Can you smell the bullshit on this report, Corporal? I'll wash my hands to remove the smell from this clipboard."

"Sir?"

"Corporal, do you know what I found outside the back door?"

"No, Sir, I haven't been out back yet."

"You haven't been out back yet? That's interesting because if you had inspected and secured the perimeter first, you would have

83

discovered the pile of cigarette butts on the ground. Someone is taking a hell of a lot of smoke breaks, and the same lazy-ass can't even properly dispose of his butts. Corporal, I visited many facilities, and initially, this was one of the most unsatisfactory surprise inspections I have conducted this entire quarter. I look forward to discovering what else I find. Let me see the inventory folder."

"Yes, Sir." The Corporal turned, opened a desk drawer, withdrew the folder, and offered it to Randy. Randy took it and began to flip through the pages as the Corporal nervously watched.

"Follow me," Randy ordered as he walked to the warehouse.

"Yes, Sir."

They stepped into the warehouse. The Corporal turned on the lights. Slowly walking up and down the aisles with the corporal close behind, Randy inspected the stacks of boxes and crates.

"I want the side of these pallets to be parallel with the yellow lines, straight, and evenly spaced inside the yellow lines. Nothing is to be touching the yellow lines."

"Yes, Sir."

"Corporal, what do you know about those sections, one through five?"

"Sir, all I know is we place specifically ordered supplies there. The numbers on the sections correspond to the cargo crates in the yard. Every month, we fill the orders and pack the crates on a schedule, then Chinooks take them away and return with empties."

"And that's all you need to know. That office looks like a damn college dormitory room. Clean it."

"Yes, Sir."

"Corporal, to my strong disagreement, I've been told that an initial inspection will be free, meaning it doesn't go into an official report. But when I return, whatever I find will be reported with names, ranks, and serial numbers. And if I were you, I wouldn't open my big mouth to anyone about this inspection because you have very little to be proud of. Am I clear on my expectations?"

"Crystal clear, Sir."

"Then why the hell are you still standing here? Get that office cleaned."

Salutes were exchanged before Randy tucked the clipboard under his arm, walked out the back door, and got into the vehicle to manipulate the wires he had exposed earlier that morning. He assumed the soldier was frantically cleaning the office. The car started, and he drove up to the gate, which began to slide open. It seemed to Randy that it took a very long time.

As he drove down the dark road, Randy grinned, shook his head in disbelief, and whistled a long note. Surprised that he had gotten away with it, he realized that he probably couldn't return to Casper Island the same way he had come. His thoughts shifted to form a new plan.

Randy quickly searched for a place to ditch the car. He understood that each step of his plan needed to be as brief and distinct as possible to make it harder for anyone to trace his actions. Various types of information can confuse anyone trying to follow him. He chose to drive out to a rural area.

Eventually, Randy found an old dirt road, drove the car to the end, and then into the woods, where it got stuck, with his tires spinning in the mud. Before removing the BDUs, Randy took out the lug wrench, dug a hole about fifty yards away, and dropped them in. After wiping off his fingerprints from the tools, he also discarded the items into the hole and refilled it. After walking back to the car, he wiped down any areas where his fingerprints might be visible, and then He removed tree branches and gathered dead leaves to cover the car completely. Finally, he took off his military beret and placed it in his bag with his water bottle and the two radios. He figured it would be a while before a hiker or hunter found the car, and by then, he would be long gone. After he finished, he walked back down the dirt road to the paved road to catch a ride.

Randy had never gone hitchhiking, but the process seemed simple enough. When he saw a vehicle approaching, he stuck out his thumb and walked backward. After forty-five minutes, he was still walking with his small bag. He noticed the sign advertising a truck stop in the next town.

Finally, a car slowed and stopped, and the driver rolled down his window as he ran to the car.

"Where are you going?"

Randy lowered his head to look at the young man and spoke with a slightly accented French. "Hello. I am just going to the truck stop diner. I had to drop off my rig at the shop."

"Get in."

As Randy walked to the other side, the driver reached over to throw a few things from the passenger seat to the back. Randy got in, and the driver continued down the road.

"Why didn't you just take a cab?"

"No. I don't get much exercise; I always drive, so walking does me good. But after a few miles, I'm ready for a ride."

"If I may ask, do I detect an accent?"

"Yes. French. My parents are from Quebec. They came over when I was thirteen. My relatives there tease me when we talk on the phone. They say I have lost my French sound."

"Well, I can hear that you still have some of it," the driver said, grinning.

"Thank you. I'll let my family know the next time they tease me."

Nothing else was said until the driver pulled into the truck stop and came to a halt. "There you go. Good luck with your rig."

"Thanks a lot. I appreciate it."

Randy got out, and the car continued through the parking lot to the other entrance, then proceeded down the road.

Randy met truck drivers at various truck stops. After a series of rides with truck drivers, using different accents and telling separate stories about himself, Randy arrived in Los Angeles. He was painfully hungry and exhausted and needed some serious personal hygiene. He knew where he wanted to go, but didn't know how to get there. Additionally, he had no money.

He didn't take long to gather a good amount of loose change and a few dollar bills while sitting on the city sidewalk with his homemade 'homeless vet' sign, wearing his beret. He felt guilty about being an impostor since he wasn't in the military anymore, yet he was following a military phrase: "Adapt and overcome."

A generous woman stopped before him, opened her lunch bag, and handed him a homemade sandwich. "Here you go, Sir. You look hungry," she said sweetly. Randy thanked her and devoured it as she walked away.

When he figured he had enough money for a cab, he counted it. Noticing another jobless man sitting near the corner, Randy realized that the man hadn't collected much money. Randy gave him his beret and sign.

"Here. These seem to work well."

The older homeless man slowly took the beret, put it on his head, laid his sign down, and held up the new one.

"Thanks."

One of the donors observing the exchange bent down and retrieved his dollar from the bucket, appearing disappointed.

Turning back toward the street, Randy hailed a cab. "How much will it cost to take me to the LA Report?" Randy asked as he bowed and looked at the cab driver through the side passenger window.

"About nineteen dollars. Maybe twenty," the driver replied. "But you'll have to pay it upfront. Sorry. I can't take the chance. You don't exactly look like a successful businessman."

"Will you take me for $17.45?"

The cab driver looked at him with hesitation. "This time. But next time, it'll be full fare. You're lucky you caught me in between the breakfast and lunch rushes. Anyway, you seem to need a break."

Randy reached through the window with his cupped hands full of coins and single-dollar bills. The driver sighed and cupped his hands to take them, saying, "Not exactly what I had in mind, but money is money. Get in."

"Thank you," Randy replied as he opened the back door and got in. He hadn't seen his reflection in days, so he glanced in the rearview mirror and rubbed his face to feel the prickly growth. With his beard growth and wrinkled clothes, he wondered if they would allow him into the building he was heading to.

At the front door of the LA Report, Randy got out of the cab. "Thanks again."

Before he drove away, the cab driver said, "You're welcome, buddy. I hope your luck changes soon, and you get the job." He nodded toward the building. "I've heard it's a good place to work, and they're good people to work with."

"Let's hope so."

Randy Meets the Bulldog

Randy walked into the building and approached the receptionist's desk, his bag smelling as bad as he looked. His appearance starkly contrasted with the clean lobby and the professional-looking people who frequented and worked there. The uniformed security guard in the lobby walked over and stopped near him.

The receptionist asked, "Hi. May I help you?"

"Yes," Randy replied. "I would like to see Margaret Stedman. Is she still the editor?"

"Yes, she is. And you are?"

"I'm Randy Dickensen. A friend of Dr. Sydney Morgan."

"Of course you are. One moment."

She pushed the button on the phone. "Ms. Stedman, I have a gentleman here who wants to see you. He said he's a friend of Dr. Morgan… Okay, I'll send him up in five minutes."

The Security Guard walked over to look in Randy's bag. "Sir, I must see what's inside before you go up the stairs. Why don't you open that up for me?"

"Sure," Randy answered as he pulled the bag open.

The security guard looked inside. "An empty water bottle and… what are those?"

"Radios."

"They're fancy ones. Turn one on for me." Randy took out a radio, turned it on, and turned the tuner left and right. The static proved that it was just a functioning radio.

"Okay. Are you a military man?"

"You might say that."

The guard smiled. "So was I. What's your M.O.S.? Rank?"

"I'm sorry, but I can't share that information with you. I could tell you a lie, but you seem like the man who would see right through it." Randy nodded his head. "You know…" He maintained firm eye contact to reinforce his claim with confidence.

"Oh, I get it," the Security Guard grinned. "You're one of 'those' Special Forces guys. You would never know it by your appearance, but I guess that's why you have to look like you do." The Security Guard leaned closer and lowered his voice. "An operative, I bet." Randy didn't reply.

"I know, you can't say," the Security Guard said, shaking his head. "You guys are something else. Thanks for what you do. I hope they pay you a lot."

"We don't do what we do just for the money, but it helps."

The guard's added enthusiasm made him sound a bit dorky. "I think it's awesome when they say that you guys don't run 'from' a fight; you run 'to' one," the guard said with an excited smile. You can have a seat over there by the water cooler.

"Thank you."

Randy sat patiently, drinking cup after cup of water until the receptionist notified him that he could go to the Editor's office.

After knocking on the door, Randy heard a voice from inside. "Come in."

Randy opened the door and stepped in. Margaret looked him up and down. "Thanks for seeing me, Ms. Stedman."

"You're welcome. Please, have a seat. I'll come around my desk to join you. So, you're a friend of Dr. Morgan?"

"Yes, but you can't let him know I'm here. He asked me not to let him know my plans. Ms. Stedman, I came to you because I was told you have the courage and secrecy to handle what I must tell you. But mostly I came because you're a friend of Dr. Morgan's. And because I trust him, I'm going to trust you."

"Ok. So, who are you?"

"My name is Randy Dickensen. I'm one of the survivors of the Advanced Soul Project."

Margaret was somewhat shocked. "What? There weren't any survivors of the ASP. They were reported to have died of some infection."

"That's what the government said. Dr. Morgan knows it isn't true because he and his team visit our prison island every month. There are seventeen of us there, and four other secret communities like ours where Caspers are held. Our island is surveilled by the Coast Guard and drones, surrounded by electronic buoys, and evidently in a no-fly zone."

"Caspers?" Margaret asked.

"I'm sorry. It's an acronym for 'Community of Advanced Soul Project. A community is called a 'Casp,' and the nickname for each inmate is a 'Casper.'"

"So, how did you get here from there?"

"It's a long story, but I smuggled myself off the island."

"Excuse me." Margaret stood and returned to the front of her desk, where she picked up her phone. "Cindy, code six."

"Right away, Margaret," came the faint reply.

"May I ask what a code six is?" Randy asked, slightly alarmed.

"It's code for my staff. Essentially, it means that you aren't here and never were. Every staff member has specific procedures to follow. It's an unwritten code we haven't used in a long time," she said with a brief, distant look.

"I like that," Randy replied with a smile. "You can't exactly put those things in a company's SOP manual."

At that moment, the receptionist, Cindy, erased the entry from the visitor's log on the computer and whispered, "Code Six" to the security guard. His part was to claim that he had never met Randy. Cindy began to make calls within the building. The IT department erased the video from the cameras in the parking lot and lobby. Cindy took a bottle of cleaner and wiped down the door handles, the countertop, and the water cooler, then collected the cups in the wastebasket to hide them.

"I just can't believe Dr. Morgan is working for the ASP," Margaret said.

"He isn't. He's working *with* them to oversee our welfare. We want to end our exile and come home. We're not dangerous, but we're not normal either. Some of us emerged from that procedure damaged, while most have developed extraordinary abilities. The government is afraid of us, but more afraid that the public will find out about us."

"Oh, a battle with the government. I have some experience with that. What can I do?"

"Well, the first record is everything I'm telling you. Please keep it to yourself for now. I must be back on the island before the middle of the month, before Dr. Morgan's team arrives. We're going to set up a satellite dish. From there, we will try hacking into some systems and telling the world these big secret lies. They'll have to bring all of us back. Ms. Stedman, I want to leave you out of this for your sake. The LA Report is just my backup plan, a plan B in case something goes wrong with plan A. But as part of Plan B. I need to give this to you." He opened his bag and took out one of the radios. "Here, I have one, too. They're the military's best. Hopefully, the signal will reach a long distance between here and the island. I'm keeping my fingers crossed for some transmission relay station."

"Randy, although I appreciate your concern for us, please know that I would love to open this can of worms if and when necessary. I'll retire soon and would love to go out with another huge story. Lately, I've grown tired of our reporting, which is mostly focused on politics, crime, and the weather. I thought I would never say this, but I'm ready for another fight, so throw this old bulldog a big bone if you need to."

Randy grinned. "Old bulldog?"

Margaret pointed to the brass bulldog on her desk. "It was an award I received a long time ago when I was a reporter. I'm tenacious when I sink my teeth into something."

"Thank you for the offering. You would be a great ally. I want to reiterate that Dr. Morgan is a great man and one of my favorites. He's protected us and made our lives better. I'm certain he's only involved in monitoring our health and safety because what's been done is done. So, what I'm thinking is that if you don't hear from me in one month, the story is yours to publish. Also, I need to know what island Casp 5 is on. May I use your internet? The airplanes dropping off the monthly cargo crates seem to come from the south and return northeast."

"Randy. Is anyone in your group good at hacking?"

"I'm not sure if anyone is good enough, but we're sure as hell going to try. Someone on the island may pick up our SOS signal from one of my radios. Hopefully, the good guys." He shrugged his shoulders, betraying his lack of confidence in that final part of the plan.

"Sure. But if you don't mind, that sounds a little weak. I'd hate to see the whole plan ruined at the last phase. With a grin, Ms. Stedman said, "Please hold on a moment."

Ms. Stedman went to her phone again but pushed a button. "Georgina, would you have a few minutes? I have a visitor who needs some help... Thanks, we'll be right down. Randy, let's take a walk. I want to introduce you to our IT Director. She's been with me for years and is 'the' best."

They descended the stairs and took a left at the receptionist's desk. The Security Guard, who had also been notified of code six, waited in the lobby, smiling at them and stabbing his finger at Randy in an 'I knew it!' manner, while sliding an invisible zipper across his mouth; he winked. Randy grinned and returned a thumbs-up.

Margaret and Randy continued down the hall to the second door on the right, then down another stair and through a door. A beautiful, smiling woman wearing a colorful dress, large earrings, several necklaces, and numerous bracelets met them as they walked into the room, which featured seven different computer systems. Massive monitors lined the wall, and two other employees sat at their stations, each with their monitors. Randy looked at them and hesitated.

"They're okay. They work for me, and I trust them. Georgina, this is Randy. Randy, this is Georgina." They exchanged 'hellos' and shook hands. "Georgina, I'll fill you in on all the details later, but we need your excellent skills now. We want to find a little island about a two-hour flight somewhere southwest of here."

Randy added, "A Chinook helicopter can fly a maximum of just over three hundred miles per hour, so I estimate, with cargo, it flew about two fifty to two hundred and seventy-five miles per hour. So, in a two-hour flight, we're looking at roughly five hundred to five hundred and fifty miles. I was on this flight, but I was in a dark box. We're looking for a small island compound with only two rows of ten square buildings and a beach. The rows are spaced about thirty feet apart. And a larger bamboo building at the end has a thatched roof."

Georgina sat down at one of her computers. "Well, let me see what I can do. How about I tap into some weather satellites, to begin with?" Her ring-covered fingers flew over her keyboard, and her bracelets rattled as different images appeared and disappeared. Suddenly, an image of the Earth formed on the screen. After finding the general vicinity, she directed the satellite with a joystick while tapping keys and saying, "Down..., down..., over..., down more..., over..., Now focus..., there! It's a small island with buildings set up just like you described! I'll put it on the wall."

Randy closely studied the huge monitor and the island.

"That's not it, but it's very close. There's no community center. You might have just found one of the other Casper communities. Can you mark the coordinates?"

"Yep. I already got these. Let's keep looking." Even with her long, painted fingernails, Georgina rapidly tapped the keys until she found the next tiny island and zoomed in to place the image on the wall monitor.

"Is this the one?" Georgina asked.

"Yes! That's it!" Randy leaned in and pointed his finger at the screen. "See the community center and the garden? And that darker square is the other clearing for the orchard. That's number five. That's where I came from. At some time, can you find the rest of them?"

"Let's do that now," Margaret suggested. "That way, we can write the coordinates down for you."

"You read my mind," Georgina replied, smiling.

It took some time, but Georgina found the three other Casper islands and wrote the coordinates on paper. "Here you go." She handed the paper to Randy.

He silently read it and handed it back. "Thanks."

"Oh, you can keep it," Georgina insisted.

"I have kept it." He tapped his head with his finger. "Right up here."

"Hmmm, charming and bright," she replied flirtatiously.

He looked at Margaret. "I must ask a huge favor. It's more like a massive imposition. I need to get back on the island without anyone knowing it. I have just under a week before Dr. Morgan's team arrives."

Margaret smiled. "By air or sea?"

"Maybe both. And we could use you, Georgina. Just know that you might at least be on the edge of illegal if that's alright."

"Honey, I live on the edge of illegal, right on the corner of Shady Street, and I Can't Believe I Just Got Through That Security Wall Avenue."

Everyone laughed as the two assistants sitting at their desks turned and smiled, nodding their heads deeply.

Georgina turned to them. "Hey, you two. Don't forget that you live just across the street from where I live. We're neighbors." Everyone laughed again.

"So, what's your plan, Randy?" Margaret asked. "I'll need a small airplane to fly me into the no-fly zone. I'll need the beacons turned off or their signals scrambled at the right time. When the warning comes over the radio, the pilot can apologize. I'll parachute into the water in scuba gear with an underwater propeller and go to the island. The airplane then leaves the zone, looking like a 'no harm, no foul' situation."

"Sounds easy enough," Margaret replied with obvious sarcasm. "Let's make up a believable story of why the airplane wandered into the zone… How about it's looking for something?"

Randy turned to Georgina, "Georgina, I'll need you to be here on standby. We'll use radios with codes hidden in our plain conversation. Do you think you can interrupt those communication buoys?"

She placed her hands on her hips and wiggled her head in confidence. "Darling, I can get them to sing the national anthem in three-part harmony."

Margaret said, "I know nothing about hacking. How do you do that hacking thing, Georgina?"

"OK. So…" She placed her wiggling fingers out in front of her and touched each one with each step in her explanation. "So basically, I send a message that goes through multiple servers worldwide. However, I designed it to split at each server, where both fragments take on new names and addresses while being hidden within other data streams until the command is completely fragmented and scattered into many small pieces. At the end of the trail, all the pieces find their way back to the part from which they were split, and the command is reassembled, essentially reversing the process, and it's delivered. If I need a reply or anything else, the information returns the same way. That's all. Sometimes, I do it alone, and sometimes, I get help from my two "neighbors" sitting over there." She winked. "In any case, there's a lot of code."

"That's all there is to it? I just got a headache trying to follow that. I have an acquaintance who's a pilot and owes me some favors. He's a 'thrill-seeker' type. I'll give him a call," Margaret announced.

"One last thing, Georgina. May I have your private email and IP address? The more information I have, the better chance I'll have," Randy said.

"Oh, my! A handsome guy, but not looking so handsome, is asking for my IP address! That's a 'score' for a geeky nerd like me!" She told him the information. He repeated it out loud and thanked her.

"My code name will be 'Darling,'" she announced. "That way, I can hear you call me Darling!"

Randy smiled. "Mine will be Hitchhiker."

Margaret announced, "Mine is 'Ed.'"

Everyone laughed lightly, even with the tension of knowing the dangerous plan they were about to begin.

Before Randy exited Margaret's car at the airport to meet up with her pilot, he thanked her. "Oh, I want to tell you that if you hear about a military car being abandoned and found, that was me. Or if you catch wind of someone impersonating a US military officer at the storage facility where the Casper's cargo crates are, that was also me."

"You mean to tell me that I'm sitting next to a felon?" Margaret teased as she suddenly leaned away from him.

"Yes. However, the list of my crimes isn't yet complete. I'll have to alphabetize them to keep track at this pace."

"Good luck, Randy. We'll be waiting to hear from you." She hugged him. "One last thing…" She reached into her purse and took out a cell phone. "This is a disposable cell phone with lots of time on it. My phone number is on the back. If I read you correctly, you want to use your government's radio in your plan against them, but only as a last resort, or if necessary. Remove the card, wipe my prints, and remove my number."

"Thanks again, Margaret. And remember, if you don't hear back from me within thirty days, please share our story with the world. I promised my Casper family that one way or another, I would make sure they got to go home even if I didn't."

"You got it."

Returning For The Rescue

Randy struggled to get his stolen scuba gear on in the tight space behind the pilot's seat. The pilot had the coordinates and was flying southwest toward Casper Island number 5 in a large zig-zag pattern to make it appear as though he was searching for something. He glanced over his shoulder and raised his voice above the engine's sound.

"I don't know what all this is about, but when Margaret Stedman tells you to keep your big mouth shut and not ask questions, guess what you say right back to her?"

"What's that?" Randy asked, finally managing to zip up his wetsuit.

"You don't say anything. You keep your big mouth shut and don't ask questions. We're about twenty minutes from the no-fly zone, and I'm sure someone is watching us."

"We can bet on that." Randy took his radio. "Darling, that balloon shouldn't be too far ahead with the wind's speed and direction. That helium doesn't last forever, so I'm flying lower. Over."

"Just keep trying to spot it. Kala's whole class is waiting to hear how far it went. Thank you for doing this. You'll be the school hero. Over," Georgina's voice replied.

Twenty-five minutes later, an authoritative voice came through the airplane's radio. "Pilot heading southwest, two hours from southern California, you have entered a restricted area. Do not proceed. I repeat. Do not proceed. Turn your aircraft off your course immediately."

Randy got back on his radio. "Darling, I've spotted the balloon floating in the water and marked the coordinates. It went a long way! I gotta head back now. Over."

"Thank you so much! See you back here. Kala said, "Thank you." Georgina replied.

With the airplane's radio, the pilot replied to the warning, "My apologies. I'm just looking for a helium balloon school project. Reversing my course as directed."

That last phrase was a cue for Georgina. Randy looked through the pilot's binoculars at the blinking beacons. Moments later, they stopped blinking. He patted the pilot on the shoulder and slid open the side door as the wind rushed by. Before he jumped out, he pushed out the green fiberglass underwater propeller and watched until its unfolding parachute was fully deployed.

The airplane banked around and returned before Randy glided to the water. Although the aircraft wasn't high enough for a safe water landing, his parachute fully opened just a minute before impact, and his entrance into the water was hard. While treading water and trying to recover, Randy stuffed the two parachutes into his bag, grasped the handles of the underwater propeller, and glided it through the water about twenty feet below the surface. As he passed between two buoys, he hoped they stayed offline until he got to the beach.

Stepping back onto the shore at Casper Island number 5, Randy immediately dragged the underwater propeller up to the beach and onto the trail. He took off his tanks and covered everything with palm branches and sand. That will have to do for now, he decided before reminding himself that Dr. Morgan and his team would arrive three days from now. Randy took out his radio from the sealed plastic bag. "Darling, tell Ed I'm coming home. Over."

Moments later, the reply came back, "Great. He'll be glad to hear it. Over."

Randy noticed the lights on the surveillance buoys flickered a few times before returning to their regular blinking pattern. "I love you, my crazy Georgina," he whispered.

The Caspers had gathered at the community center for lunch. The routine conversations were quieter than usual as everyone thought about Randy, Dennis, and their fates. Suddenly, they heard a Russian accent voice shouting, "Is there anything left?! I'm starving!" Randy stood in his black hooded wetsuit just outside the trail entrance. While running over to him, Bear barked and bared his long teeth. When Bear got in front of the stranger, he wagged his tail and cried, nudging him with his nose. Everyone stopped talking as they turned to look at the mysterious intruder. No one recognized him with his heavy whiskers and the unfamiliar accent. Randy knew this and extended the mystery to the hushed group for fun. Still, in a Russian accent, he yelled again, "Hello! How is everyone?! Nice to meet you! I only stopped by for lunch and some vodka! I haven't got much time because I must catch the next whale in about fifteen minutes! What do you have to eat?! Smells delicious!"

Alarmed at the sight of the intruder, Sebastian, Charlie, and Landon stood. Landon took the iron poker from the fire pit, and they all started walking right over to the stranger.

"Who are you, and what are you doing here?" Charlie demanded as they approached.

Randy waited until the three stern-faced men were standing in front of him. He reached up, pulled off his hood, and laughed loudly. He replied in his voice, "I'm an escaped convict. My name is Randy."

Instantly, the group erupted in noisy chatter and rushed toward him. But getting close enough to give hugs and kisses was hard because his three brave friends wouldn't let him go. After everyone had their turn, they helped him remove his gear and escorted him to an eating table.

Over the next several hours, he told them the story, often interrupted by questions and the laughter of disbelief, especially when he imagined himself as an army officer chewing out a surprised corporal. Randy told them at the end of the story, "We have to bury all the scuba gear deep somewhere." Charlie and Sebastian volunteered. He reminded them all that in just three days, Dr. Morgan and the others would arrive to take Dennis back to the ASP two weeks after that if the crate Randy had filled with the equipment wasn't discovered, the monthly cargo crate would include the items necessary to build a satellite to link with the media.

The Ring of Life Energy

The Coast Guard ship was finally spotted on the horizon, but it was unnecessary to inform the community until it anchored about a half-mile out. When the ship eventually arrived at its regular place, it stopped. Marsha walked up the trail and informed Randy, who rang the bell four times. Some Caspers emerged from their homes, while others came up from the fish traps, the garden, or from attending to the animals. Eventually, almost everyone met at the beach where the rubber rafts always landed.

Randy noticed the second uniform at the front of the raft and whispered to Landon, "There's an additional guard this time. Igor brought an armed sailor. They must be deadly serious about their plan to take Dennis back."

Landon put his hand on Randy's shoulder. "Oh, they're gonna try, but they'll have to get through us first."

Dr. Morgan stepped over the side of the boat with everyone else. He was smiling as he walked up the beach. He paused to pet Bear and gave him a dog biscuit before he shook hands with Randy, Charlie, Landon, and the others.

"It's good to see all of you again."

"And it's great to see you too," Randy replied with a smile as Dr. Morgan's team filed past them with smiles and greetings, making their way to the community center to set up for the tests and examinations. The four men fell in behind them.

"So, how are things since I last saw you?" Dr. Morgan asked with his customary concern before he sipped his coffee at a table in the pavilion.

Randy looked across the table at him. "Things have been solidly routine. We've planted some trees and are almost complete with the fish farm. There are just a couple more nets to put up. The chickens seem to be happy. Since there are no predators except the occasional raptor, they wander off in the morning and return to roost just before dark. The horses are fine with the hay from the cargo crates, but the goats don't like to stay in their pen. We assure them we know how it feels."

"Good. Listen. Randy, I think I know you well enough to say that there's something wrong," Dr. Morgan whispered.

Randy's countenance got serious, and he whispered, "Dr. Morgan, they're not taking Dennis while the rest of us are still standing. We have all had enough of the ASP testing and experiments. Since Dennis cannot protect himself, resist, or even realize what's happening, the rest of us will protect him. You find a safe place off to the side when the guards come for him. We'll offer peaceful resistance at first."

"Well, thanks for the warning. I assumed as much and never intended to be part of taking Dennis. Just remember, they have guns, and you don't. Randy, we're not leaving for a few hours yet, so let's visit and talk about the other issues until then. OK?"

"Sure. How about my requests?" Randy asked.

"I didn't bring them this time, but the request was granted. I didn't bring them because there was a stipulation, as I thought there would be. And I was right; they wanted to install observation cameras. But as of this time, they're leaving the choice up to you: electricity or privacy. I need to see what the group decides before we go further."

Randy replied, "We already talked about it and decided that we're going to turn it down. I must tell you personally that the mood has soured around here with this whole thing. The tide seemed to have completely turned when the government decided to take us back for more experimentation or whatever the hell else they wanted to do. And now we've been denied some basic comforts because we don't want the jackasses back in Washington intruding on our privacy. This situation is what it is, so they could conceal their experimental mistakes while wanting to do even more experiments."

"I empathize with you. I do. Your feelings are not unreasonable."

Scarlett walked up to them, holding a carafe. "Sorry to interrupt, but would you gentlemen like another cup of coffee?"

"Yes. Just warm it up, please," Dr. Morgan replied, lifting his cup. He looked over at the line of Caspers. There were just three more to go, including Randy, who always liked to go last. In case something happened to one of the others, he could intervene or help.

Randy's exam finished, and the team began to pack their equipment. He walked over to stand by Dr. Morgan and looked around at the scene, deciding that the time had come. Tension started to fill the air. The guards didn't know what to expect, and the Caspers would do their best to see that Dennis wasn't taken. Nervous glances and slight nods from the other Caspers suggested they were ready.

"Excuse me, Dr. Morgan. It's time," Randy announced before he walked over to the bell and rang it once.

101

Joanne carefully escorted Dennis to the middle of the clearing in front of the pavilion and stood with him. The rest of the Caspers walked over to form a loose circle around him. Everyone faced Randy's back because they knew that was where the confrontation would begin.

Jim and the sailor walked over to Dr. Morgan. Jim said, "Doc, we have our orders. Dr. Br..." Jim gave a regretful look at his slip of the tongue.

"Dr. Brown? So, you answer to Dr. Brown. I know Jim. Be as gentle as you can."

Dr. Morgan's nervous team saw the circle and concluded that something bad was about to happen. The doctors, nurses, and technicians quickly packed their things and returned to the beach.

The two guards walked over near Randy. Jim stepped up in front of him. "C'mon, Randy, you know I must do my job. I have orders to take Dennis back."

"Not today, Jim. If Dennis were your brother and you loved him as we do, you would be standing with us instead of opposed to us."

Jim tried to brush past him, but Randy pushed him away. He nodded his head up and down. "OK. If that's the way you want it!" He grabbed Randy by the shoulders, trying to wrestle him to the side. Randy quickly brought up his arms between Jim's arms, breaking his hold, and punched him hard in the face, followed by a quick spinning back kick that landed squarely in the middle of Jim's chest, knocking him back and onto the ground. After lying on his back for a few moments, Jim got back up, pulled out his sidearm, and pointed it at Randy. The Sailor with him drew his weapon, too.

Charlie, Landon, and Sebastian raised their fists. Some of the women also did so. It was an ineffective act against bullets, but it clearly showed intention.

Dr. Morgan raised his voice to be heard, "Jim, are you sure you want to shoot unarmed American citizens?"

"Damn it! I have my orders! By any means necessary, one way or the other, Dennis is going back with us."

The Caspers determined that neither of the soldiers would be able to reach Dennis. Instinctively, the Caspers strengthened their circle by joining hands to fill in the gaps between them and braced themselves. When the last two hands were joined, an ethereal hum rose from the circle. Natasha, Dr. Morgan, and a few others had heard it before in the garden, but it was much louder this time. The hum was followed by a bright, light-blue ring that formed to rest above the Caspers' heads. Thousands of tiny strands of colors swam freely within the ring as smiling faces watched in awe. Small flares stretched out and receded. Next, a thin dome of translucent blue energy formed above the ring, producing a large flare at the top that suddenly reached down to envelop Dennis, covering him for a few moments, and then lifted itself back up. The bewildered guards took some steps back and stared in fear and confusion.

Dr. Morgan stood where he was, also staring in wonderment. He knew they were witnessing a circuit of life energy.

Joanne stood with Dennis in the middle and was the first to notice Dennis slowly turning his head. He looked around with awareness in his eyes for the first time since the ASP procedure. After walking over to the others, he gently gripped Tyron's and Marshall's hands and pulled them apart to join the circle as his friends displayed surprised and happy faces. The volume of the hum and the brightness of light in the ring increased slightly. Joanne smiled, teared up, and joined the circle, which again increased the volume of the hum and the intensity of the light. Everyone in the circle looked at each other and up at the ring, smiling and gazing with joy. Sitting beside Dr. Morgan, Bear stared at the ring with his ears up, tilting his head back and forth.

Jim and the other sailor distanced themselves from the circle of Caspers. "Commander Sir, we have a situation," Jim informed the Coast Guard ship through his radio.

"What's the situation?"

"Sir, this will sound crazy, but the Caspers have some weird glowing electrical force."

"Is there any danger?"

"Unknown, Sir," Jim replied.

"Let me speak with Dr. Morgan."

"Aye, Sir. Stand by." Jim wiped the blood from his mouth as he walked over to Dr. Morgan with Randy's dirty boot print still on the front of his uniform. He handed the radio to Dr. Morgan. "Doc, the Commander would like to speak with you."

"Hello, Commander, this is Dr. Morgan. Over"

"Dr. Morgan, what is your assessment of the situation? Over."

"There's no apparent danger from the Caspers. The only danger that I can see is two sailors pointing their weapons at seventeen unarmed citizens who refused to give up one of their own. That code, I'm sure, is something you understand. Over."

The Commander replied, "Doctor, I don't know anything about this island or its inhabitants, so I'll consider whatever advice you have. You're the expert. Over."

Dr. Morgan again spoke into the radio. "I advise Jim and the sailor to stand down and return to the ship as scheduled without the subject. I can't predict what might happen if they don't. A very unusual natural phenomenon occurs here, and everyone is on edge. Commander, I'll take responsibility from there if we can agree. Over"

"Agreed, Dr. Morgan. Please let me speak again to that sailor. Over."

"Jim, he wants to speak with you." Dr. Morgan handed the radio back to him.

"Aye, Sir…. understood. Over and out."

Jim turned to Dr. Morgan. "We've been ordered to stand down and return to the ship without Dennis." He pointed at the glowing ring and circle of Caspers. "Good luck with those," he said with a tone of sarcasm. "I always knew that someday these freaks would hurt someone."

"Jim, you started a fight with another man and got hurt. That's the only injury that happened here today. Keep that straight. I'll see you on the beach in a few minutes. Now get going."

Jim and the sailor walked back to the beach, periodically looking over their shoulders at the energy ring and shaking their heads. The back of Jim's uniform was dirty from getting knocked to the ground.

Dr. Morgan walked over to Randy, still holding hands with the rest of the circle.

"Are you alright?"

"Couldn't be happier," Randy said, smiling. "My hand hurts a little, but other than that, I'd say things went pretty well." The other Capers agreed by making short comments.

"Before you all let go of each other's hands, I'd like to see what happens if I step in."

Dr. Morgan separated Randy's and Charlie's wrists to join the circle. Instantly, the hum stopped, and the ring of life energy vanished, but not before Dr. Morgan experienced a flash of energy.

"Wow, that felt wonderful! But I guess the disappearing ring says something about me since I'm not one of you. Now, retake each other's hands without me." The hum returned, and the energy ring formed over their heads. "I thought that would happen."

Dr. Morgan looked down the path to ensure Jim and the sailor were out of sight. "Well, it seems you all are safe now. You can release each other's hands. Then, he walked over to Dennis, who followed the Doctor with his eyes. "Dennis, I'm Doctor Morgan. How are you?"

"It seems that I'm much better. Maybe I'm better now. Maybe even better than I've ever been! That hum got inside me, and the energy flowed over my head and down to my feet. I could feel it swimming inside me." He looked around at the trees and up to the sunny sky. "It's good to be alive again." Looking down at his pants, he reached down and felt the bulge. "Uh, why am I wearing a diaper?" Finally, he looked at the smiling people around him and asked, "And who are these people?"

"Dennis, I want you to know that you have a lot of loving friends here. They took great care of you for a year, and you're the reason for this Caper's circle of friends. They protected you with their lives just now," Dr. Morgan answered.

The Caspers smiled, nodded, and took turns hugging Dennis and introducing themselves.

"Randy, I'm sure today will cause a lot more commotion back at Washington, especially after Jim submits his report to Dr. Brown and they view the recording from his helmet cam. I'll try to reduce the sensationalism in my report, but it won't be easy. I imagine there will be some unexpected visits. Everyone should relax and go back to their daily routines. Walk me back to the boat?"

"Of course," Randy replied.

The two men headed down between the buildings to the beach, leaving behind exciting conversations.

"Although I'll never forget this extraordinary day, Randy, things will change for this community significantly."

Because Randy trusted Dr. Morgan to keep things confidential, he replied, "And the other four communities, too."

Dr. Morgan abruptly stopped and turned to Randy. "Randy! How did you find out about them?"

"Let's just say for now that a little birdie told me. And now it's on my shoulders to protect them all."

"Is there anything I can do?" Dr. Morgan asked in a lowered voice.

"Just act surprised when the whole thing is blown open."

"That'll be easy because I have no idea what you have in mind. Randy, expect the worst at any time. I must remind you that some folks back in Washington want to make all this disappear. With this... well, I seriously hope you have a plan, Randy. But knowing you, you've had one for a long time. What can I do? Maybe I'll put some extra things in the next crate."

"No. Please don't bring attention to the crate."

"Would it help if I arranged for the next shipment to arrive a week early?"

"It would help more than you know, Dr. Morgan."

"I'll make up a good reason. I'd love to ask many questions right now," Dr. Morgan said. "You can't imagine how badly."

"And I'd love to answer them, but you can't know at this juncture. It's for your good. But even so, I will ask you something else I shouldn't ask. Please ask Margaret and Ms. Georgina to monitor and possibly record every CASP through satellites if things go badly for us. I'll especially need her attention in the evening and morning after the cargo crate arrives. Also, tell Margaret to expect a radio transmission from us at the same time. She knows our story."

Dr. Morgan couldn't help but laugh out loud softly. "Randy, you astonish me. I can't wait to hear how you managed that!"

"I was in their offices this week," Randy calmly said. "I'd appreciate it if you could find some time to meet up with her as soon as possible."

To let it settle in his mind, Dr. Morgan closed his eyes for a moment to understand. "Wait. You were in Margaret Stedman's office this week. That means you left the island and got back. Find some time?! I'll make time!"

The men shook hands, and Dr. Morgan walked down the beach to the waiting boat, trying to keep a straight face.

The Caspers gathered and prepared the evening meal at the community center. They ate with exciting conversations. Randy stood and tapped his spoon on his cup at the end of the meal until the noise settled to silence. "Friends, let me first offer our welcome to Dennis." Applause and whistles rose and fell. "This afternoon, we experienced something very spectacular. Somehow, even with all our patchwork souls, or perhaps because of them, powerful life energy profoundly flowed through us. When we all held hands, it was as if an electric circuit was formed, or as if we were an antenna that just tuned in to the frequency of life itself, or perhaps our hands became a conduit for what is already inside us. After speaking with Dr. Morgan privately, I think there are two future possibilities. One is that the director of the ASP will demand to know the 'hows and whys' of what happened, and either take us all back for tests and examinations. Or, the other real possibility is they come to eradicate us as if we're some dangerous mutants. There's some good news, though: a chance for survival. Dr. Morgan will attempt to deliver our next cargo crate to us within one week. There isn't much we can do until then. But once that crate arrives, it'll be time to move quickly. From now on, we must establish a guard schedule that rotates among us all, ensuring we're always on watch in case of unexpected visitors. Two people should be on each shift: one patrolling on the beach without a flashlight and the other under the bell with a flashlight turned off. The first step is always to secure the parameter, so if anyone would like to provide an additional patrol, please do so. Two bells ring, meaning we will all quickly gather at the pavilion. We'll put together a sign-up sheet and post it for everyone to see. Thank you."

Two Good Friends

Since Dr. Morgan and Margaret Stedman had become friends, they sometimes got together for lunch. Dr. Morgan asked for this occasion today. They met outside a small restaurant on a beautiful afternoon. After exchanging greetings and a gentle hug, they were seated at a small table and handed menus by the server.

Dr. Morgan concealed his playful feelings, saying, "What a gorgeous day. Oh, and before I forget, Randy said, 'Hello,' and wants to remind you to be ready with Georgina on the evening of the next cargo crate delivery, which will be a week earlier than usual. Please continue to be ready early the next day. I don't know what that means. But let's have some lunch. I'm hungry." He put on his reading glasses, picked up a menu, and began to look for the daily special.

Margaret leaned forward in her chair with wide eyes. "You talked to him about escaping?"

"Yep. And I'm helping Randy," Dr. Morgan replied without looking up. "Boy, the fish tacos look good. Hey, you get three," Dr. Morgan casually said as he continued to study the menu. "But I'm still considering the daily special. What do you think about meatloaf? Do you like meatloaf, Margaret? I've never had it here."

"Sydney! Talk to me. It seems I know one-half, and you know the other half."

"Correction. I know a third, you know a third, and the other third, nobody knows." He didn't lift his eyes from his menu. "I've heard good things about their Reuben sandwich, though. I love sauerkraut."

Margaret caught on to the little cat-and-mouse game. "I'm sure I know much more than you do. After all, I spent hours with him in my office. I know how he got off the island, and I even helped him get back."

Dr. Morgan still hadn't lifted his eyes from the menu. "But you don't know why or what happened. That's the big news. Hey, this one comes with a pickle and fries."

"Sydney Morgan!" Margaret abruptly took his menu from his hands and laid it on the table.

"OK. I'll get serious," he said after a brief smile. He took off his glasses, leaned back, and sighed. "The government might choose to kill them all, take them all back, or at the very least, install video cameras to monitor their day-to-day activities. Or anything else in between. Currently, the Caspers have no electricity. Their only connections to the world are my visits, battery-operated radio with no English-speaking stations, old magazines, and redacted newspapers. They're doing the best they can."

"They're getting a satellite dish, you know," Margaret said.

"Doesn't surprise me. Randy seems normal on the surface, but he's brilliant, and most others have extraordinary abilities. Let me tell you what happened."

Dr. Morgan recalled the incident of the circle of Caspers and the ring of life energy to Margaret. She was astonished at the whole incident.

"So, Sydney, why are you involved with the Caspers? Why didn't you blow the lid off these secret communities initially?"

Margaret, for two reasons. First of all, you know how the government can be. What would happen to the Caspers if this got out and I couldn't manage their safety? Further, what might happen to me before I could get it out to the public?

Margaret shrugged her shoulders. "I don't know."

"Neither do I, but we know it might not end well for us. I might find myself in concrete shoes, high-diving from a helicopter ride to the sea. The second reason is that by joining the STP, I can do my best to ensure they're all safe and cared for. It's the least I can do. You know that old saying: Keep your friends close…"

Margaret finished, "And your enemies, closer."

By the end of their lunch date, they both knew what the other did. The doctor and the editor agree to work together.

On the day of the expected cargo crate delivery, just a week after Dr. Morgan's team left, the regular group of Caspers waited with their horses at the tree line. The cargo flew over the beach as the gray cargo crate fell out of the back. The big parachute opened, and the crate landed with a slight bounce on the sand. The pilot waved his wings, and the Caspers waved back. Everything happened as it did at every previous airdrop.

The horses were packed with boxes, and the team went to the community center. Before Charlie left the cargo crate, he looked up to confirm that the secret compartment was still there, but it was now packed with smaller boxes and a new replacement shovel.

Politicians and Scientists Conspire

Late at night, a car pulled into a parking space at the facility where the ASP procedures were done. Jim stepped out of the driver's seat and went around the back of the car to open the passenger door. Dr. Brown stepped out. The two of them entered the building and went to the conference room.

The three senators who sat on the secret committee overseeing the ASP, along with the six members of the ASP board, watched the video from Jim's helmet cam on a large TV. They all viewed it with excited fascination. After the video was played for the second time, the discussion around the table grew intense as they tried to determine the next step. Naturally, the ASP board was very enthusiastic about the ring of life energy and its restorative power for Dennis.

"The potential of this energy is enormous! Imagine hospitals, emergency rooms, and battlefield medics had this ability!" Dr. Brown exclaimed and pleaded with the senators. "We must bring them all back here, study them, and develop this energy!"

Senator Moseby, the chairman, offered the other side of the coin. "Having them back on the mainland would be risky. There's always the chance of them escaping. And who knows what they might do with that power in revenge for what was done to them? We just witnessed the kind of power they can produce. Maybe they can generate more. This might be the time to end the Caspers since no one knows they're even there."

Dr. Cohen offered, "If seventeen Caspers can produce that, imagine what ninety Caspers could do."

"This is a completely new source of energy that's beyond anything we know or have," Dr. Rajah noted.

Dr. Brown said, "Please, senators, what if we bring them back..."

Senator Jones raised her voice. "Dr. Brown, excuse me! You have no idea what will happen to this country if this gets out to the public! It will produce a political and social catastrophe that we have never seen! If we bring them back and your experiments fail, all you have is a failed experiment. But if we bring them back and this power is used against us, the citizens who already don't trust or like the government might finally rise."

"Yes, bringing the Caspers back has risks, but the potential benefits are multiple times greater. This power could yield tremendous international advantages in terms of finances and military strength. Nuclear energy? What was that?" Dr. Perry asked.

Calming herself, Dr. Brown carefully said, "Senators, I have a suggestion that might be acceptable to everyone. Send a group of elite military personnel to the island. The Caspers can easily be apprehended, secured, and brought back here. We'll keep them locked down and separated so they can't make that ring. If things go wrong on the island or if that energy thing is used as a weapon, give the military the right to retaliate. The worst case is that the troops bury seventeen corpses and leave."

Senator Moseby paused and looked at the other two senators, who nodded reluctantly.

"Alright. I'll notify the Coast Guard, the Army, and Dr. Morgan."

Dr. Brown gingerly offered, "Senators, if I may. Let's leave Dr. Morgan out of the loop on this one. We can't be sure how close he has become with the Caspers. How this operation goes will be very important, and it must be done correctly and without interference."

"Agreed," Senator Moseby replied.

Back at the Casp community center, the Caspers watched as Randy moved boxes around until he found the one he had packed at the military supply facility. "Finally!" Sebastian helped him carry it back to his house. Olivia needed no cue. She followed right behind them.

Inside his small concrete house, Randy opened the box. "I can't believe it's all here. Let's get busy."

The small group assembled the satellite components as quickly as possible while discussing precisely what to put in the letter. They worked until dark, when they asked volunteers to bring lanterns to the small house to hold their flashlights.

"We can't risk firing this up until it's fully charged, and we have to," Olivia said. "Someone might detect the signal or the energy."

Charlie added, "The solar panels should charge the batteries after a couple of hours."

"Okay, folks. Let's take a break. Get some sleep and meet me back here at daybreak," Randy instructed. "First, we'll set up the solar panels and hook them to the batteries. Jon and Lee, can you guys do that?"

"You got it," Jon replied.

Lee agreed. "Yep. No problem. Just make sure there's coffee."

Sharon promised to ensure there was plenty of hot coffee. "I still have four days until I have to sleep, so I'll be awake all night anyway."

"Who's on first watch tonight?" Randy asked.

"Theresa and Jon are," Marsha answered.

"Good."

"Theresa, I'll sit with you on watch if you want me to," Sharon offered.

"Yes! Thanks so much! It's so boring, sitting under the bell for four whole hours."

The Expected Visit

The next morning, the batteries charged in two hours of direct sunlight. Randy and Charlie attached the batteries to the panels and leaned them at an angle to catch the first rays as the sun peeked over the horizon. After fully charging the batteries, the others excitedly took the computer and small satellite dish outside and attached the last cables.

"Ok, Olivia, do your thing," Randy said, stepping back.

Olivia sat on a small crate at the keyboard, which rested on the empty box.

"Give me power," she said.

Sebastian flipped a switch, calling power from the batteries. Olivia turned the laptop's power button on. "Bingo," she exclaimed, anxiously waiting for the laptop to boot up. As soon as she could, she opened the word processor and typed the handwritten letter into the media they had written the previous night. The community also used the computer's camera to take a self-portrait with everyone, including Bear.

"How about that radio you brought back?" Landon asked. "Do you think it'll reach back to LA?"

"Yes. I know it will," Randy replied. "I used it from the beach when I came back. It's the newest military radio, and it's powerful enough to reach Los Angeles. I'm sure of it." He turned it on and tuned it to the channel Georgina had suggested, and he agreed.

"Darling, this is Hitchhiker. Do you copy?" He turned to the group, covered the radio with his hand, smirked, and said, "Georgina picked out her code name." Randy waited about fifteen seconds and repeated, "Darling, this is Hitchhiker. Do you copy?"

A familiar voice came back. "This is your Darling reading you loud and clear, Hitchhiker. Ed and I are just sitting here bored. Our mutual friend is here to keep us company."

Again, Randy covered the radio and said to the group. "Ed is Margaret Stedman's code name."

"Isn't she that newspaper editor?" Tyrone asked.

"The same," Randy replied. "And the 'friend' must be Dr. Morgan."

Suddenly, Bear started to bark, and the community bell rang twice. The faint sound of an approaching airplane drew everyone's attention. Heads tilted up, and hands shaded eyes that searched the sky.

"We must move on this now! Our company is on its way!" Randy spoke into the radio while looking up at the approaching airplane.

Georgina replied through the radio, "I need your computer's address." Olivia found the address and told Randy, four digits at a time. Randy relayed them to Georgina, who said, "Ok, give me a few moments to get a satellite…"

"The letter and the picture are on the desktop," Randy added.

Lee pointed up and said, "Here they come!"

The team continued looking as twenty parachutes opened above the island. Each parachute made a soft 'pop' sound.

"Military! And they have weapons!" Charlie called out.

Randy got back on the radio. "We have about twenty military parachutes coming down around the island, and they look to be in full combat gear and ready for business."

"I have a satellite link!" Georgina's hurried voice exclaimed. "I'm taking your cursor."

The Caspers watched as the parachutes disappeared behind the trees. The laptop's cursor flew around the screen.

"We haven't got much time, Darling!"

"I'm almost there. Going as fast as I can… Just… about." The rapid sound of her fingernails tapping the keys could be heard while she spoke.

Quick and heavy footsteps from every direction could be heard in the bushes and trees as combat boots crunched branches underfoot. The soldiers weren't sneaking toward the Caspers; they were hurrying to take positions.

"They're coming through the woods!" Jon said, looking around. "They're already behind us!"

"Everyone, stay put and remain calm. Let Randy do the talking," Charlie ordered as the soldiers arrived and took positions behind trees, pointing their weapons at them. The Caspers were surrounded.

Georgina came back on the radio. "I'm sending the files... There they go! I've sent your letter and group picture to the media and the Pentagon."

"Whew! They're here. I gotta go!"

Randy changed the channel, turned the radio off, broke the cell phone that Margaret had given him, and then pushed it down into the coals with the steel poker. He turned to the group. "We've had to buy time. Work with me."

As this hidden incident played out on the obscure, tiny island, media reporters and assistants to politicians around the country sat at their desks, routinely checking their email inboxes. A new email marked 'Urgent' and 'Advanced Soul Project Survivors Found!' appeared in their 'new mail' boxes. None of them wanted to be embarrassed and forced to apologize as victims of another internet prank. Some recipients who saw the title dismissed it as just tabloid spam and deleted it, while others clicked on it, read it, and then deleted it. However, some reporters, clerks, and interns re-read it before deciding to bring it to the attention of their superiors. Some bosses discredited it and chose not to take it any further. However, enough of them risked their professional integrity and immediately published it.

The picture of the Caspers grouped in front of palm trees and small cement buildings tipped the scales of their decision. A couple of people in the Pentagon knew the email was very likely genuine and scrambled desperately to assess and control the damage. Phones were snatched from their receivers, and people rushed down the halls for emergency meetings. Speechwriters for members of Congress and the President labored frantically over their word processors, trying to explain and spin the story to their advantage. Phones at the White House rang like never before as citizens called to inquire about the report's legitimacy. The operators were unaware of it and reflexively denied any knowledge of it. At lightning speed, the email became a story, a panic that evolved into a worldwide breaking news feature.

Randy gathered there with the others who depended on him, knowing he needed to buy time for the story to become a breaking news report. But this wouldn't just affect them on Casper 5. Four other Casps, oblivious to the situation at Casp 5, moved through another typical day in secret captivity.

A young Officer stepped out from the trail, flanked by the armed sailor with a weapon ready. The man on the other side was Jim, with his gun ready.

The Officer shouted, "I'm Lieutenant Witherford of the US Army! I have orders to be here! I intend to harm no one! I need to speak with Randy!"

"I'm Randy! You may approach!" Randy shouted back.

The three military men walked over to the group.

"I'll have that radio," the Lieutenant said, taking it from Randy's hand and inspecting it. "Hmm, military." Pointing to the satellite system, he ordered, "Sergeant, take that all away!"

"Yes, Sir!" The Sergeant replied from the trees and signaled two other soldiers to follow him. Three soldiers approached the satellite system. "It's military, Lieutenant. The latest," the Sergeant said." They pulled out the cables and carried away the dismantled system.

Randy looked at the soldiers at the tree line. "Williams! Monty! Is that you?!"

"Yep! How are you, Dickensen?!"

"Great! It's good to see you, men! I can't believe you got ordered to this shit detail!"

Williams shrugged his shoulders, and Monte nodded.

"Now, Randy, you're going to tell me where you got all that from," the Lieutenant said with a tone as if speaking to a child.

"Not until I speak to a lawyer."

The Lieutenant laughed mockingly. "Do you seriously think I'm taking you to a lawyer? No one remembers who you are, much less will believe your story. As I understand it, you all died. No, Randy. I'm taking all of you in handcuffs back to the hospital you were taken from. These are my orders. Our ship is just off the shore, and rubber rafts are waiting on the beach. There's a doctor lady who misses you. We shouldn't keep her waiting."

Hearing their disheartening future, something inside Dennis snapped. He lifted his shirt, took out a hidden knife, and rushed at the Officer, screaming, "I'm not going back!"

Jim shot Dennis in the leg, but because of the substantial amount of life energy in him, Dennis only stumbled briefly and continued to attack the surprised Lieutenant.

"No! Dennis!" Randy yelled.

Jim fired again. The round passed through Dennis's torso and slammed into a palm tree at the edge of the clearing. Dennis dropped to the dirt, motionless. The sailor raised his weapon and swept it back and forth at the Caspers.

"Get him a medic, for God's sake!" Charlie pleaded.

"The young Lieutenant dryly replied, "He's dead. No one survives a center-mass shot from that distance with that weapon."

Monte shouted from his position, "Buddy, if you fire another round, you're going to catch hell!"

The Lieutenant turned to the trees and shouted to his troops, "I'm in command, and I give the orders!"

Jim lowered his weapon and nervously turned to glance at the tree line. To everyone's surprise, Dennis moaned. Defying the sailor's order to 'freeze,' the Caspers instantly gathered around Dennis and formed a circle after taking each other's hands. They hoped the ring of life energy would at least be enough to prevent him from dying in the next few moments and would strengthen him. A hum began. The Lieutenant's eyes shifted back and forth as if he felt something was sneaking up on him—the light-blue ring of life energy formed above the Caspers, and the dome formed over the ring. Again, a large flare descended on Dennis, paused, and then withdrew back up. The soldiers in the trees all crouched down. The Lieutenant, Jim, and the sailor stepped back.

"Oh, I'm hurt," Dennis moaned as he clawed the dirt, lying face down.

"Dennis, just lie there and try to relax the best you can," Randy told him.

Two medics hurried over from the trees but stopped a few yards from the circle. "Lieutenant, I must try to do what I can. He might die anyway, but I have to try."

The Lieutenant reluctantly nodded in permission.

"Zeek is a damn good medic. Friends, let them through," Randy said.

The group separated their hands, and the energy ring quickly faded. The medics rapidly squeezed past the Caspers and dropped down to the ground to attend to Dennis's wounds.

"Randy, any more attacks like that, and I'll order my men to fire at will. I've got that Ace up my sleeve. I've been permitted to take it out and throw it on the table."

"Fire at Will?" Randy asked, looking confused. "Why would you want to fire weapons at Will? There's no one even here by that name. Besides, even if he were here, he didn't do anything wrong. I'll vouch for him. He's a good guy, Will is." Randy turned around to his group. "Is there anyone here named 'Will'? It might be short for William, Willy, or Wilson. When you see him, tell him to expect to be shot at, but no one knows when or why."

Again, Randy was trying to buy as much time as he could for the media to report on the letter and photo, even if it meant using an old joke. Most of the other Caspers picked up on it and looked around at each other.

"No. I don't believe there are any 'Will's here," Charlie answered. "The guy might go by the name Wilfred. But just in case, let me check." He joined his two index fingers and began offering names as he looked at the other Caspers. "When I call your names, please respond with 'here.' Let's see. We have a Marsha…"

"Here."

"A Natasha…

"Here."

"A Jose over there."

"Present!"

Charlie shook his head. "There's always one in every crowd."

"We have a Theresa."

"Here."

"How about Will?... Is there a Will? No? Sorry, I don't think he's here. Oh, wait! That's right. He just left. He said he had to get a desk and soft chair for the new Lieutenant because he isn't used to being on his feet."

Randy laughed, cueing all the Caspers to chuckle, too. The Lieutenant looked irritated as he interrupted. "Randy, you're a cocky group, given the situation you're in. What the hell was that ring of light? What kind of technology are you playing with here?"

"Believe it or not, Lieutenant, it comes from a formula we discovered in the Army after trying to make batteries in a survival training situation. You should try this sometime if you can imagine being away from your desk in BDUs. First, you mix coconut oil with kerosene. Then, you add some goat milk and bring it all to a boil. However, you can't let it boil for too long, as it won't stay in a paste form. You can't use the formula unless it's in the form of a paste. Boil it for five minutes; no more and no less. Then while it's still hot, stick all the paste right up your ass. That way, you can do your duty with your booty."

Laughter broke out among the Caspers. Even a few of the soldiers chuckled at the clever setup and delivery.

The embarrassed Lieutenant glanced over at the tree line, then took out his sidearm and pointed it at the Caspers. "You little ass-wipe. I could shoot right now," he snarled.

Williams shouted out, "Lieutenant, don't do it! You other two men, lower your weapons! Now!"

The Lieutenant turned to the tree line. "You damn SF guys think your hot shit, but you don't know a damn thing about the chain of command!" He holstered his weapon.

Jim hesitated. The sounds of rounds being chambered came from the tree line. Jim moved his weapon to his side and squatted to set it on the ground. The sailor did the same.

Randy laughed, unconcerned at the threat. "I've always wanted to say that to a fresh-out OCS Officer. Lieutenant, do you see any wires or machines around here? That was nature's concentrated life energy. I'm sure you already saw the video from Jim's helmet cam. Remember? It's the video on Jim's camera right after one of the cute kittens playing in the flower pot. That's Jim's favorite. I hope it wasn't erased. Jim dearly loves his soft kittens. So, what's next?"

Before the Lieutenant could answer, Dennis, lying between the two medics, moaned, "Randy, don't let them take us back…please."

"Dennis, they're just our ride home, that's all. There will be no more procedures, and any additional tests will be conducted on a volunteer basis. We're finally going home." All the Caspers smiled.

The Lieutenant looked at the group and said, "Just to be very clear, you're all going back to the hospital for tests, and no one knows you're even alive, nor will they!"

Randy looked at his watch. "Lieutenant, that's where you're wrong. I imagine the news has hit all over the country by now. Radio back to the ship and ask them what the latest headline in the media is. Call the Pentagon if you want. Go ahead."

"What? Do you think your Caspers are in the headlines? I'm not taking the bait."

"Randy replied, "You saw me talking on the radio, and you saw the laptop and satellite. You make the call." He pointed at the radio the Lieutenant was holding. "You can use my radio there in the fire if you like. I don't mind at all. Just make sure it's not a long-distance call. And can you try calling collect?" He shrugged his shoulders and looked behind him at the smiling faces. "Do they still even do that? You know how high the roaming charges are, Lieutenant, so try to keep the call short." Randy continued to intentionally aggravate the Lieutenant by adding every moment he could to ensure the news had hit the media.

"It's not your damn radio, and I sure as hell don't need your permission." After staring at Randy briefly, the Lieutenant replied, "So help me. You better not be yanking my chain." He turned on the radio and tuned it to the proper channel before walking away to speak privately with the ship.

Randy stood with his feet apart and his arms folded. "So, Igor, how's the jaw?" He said it loudly enough for the other soldiers to hear.

"The next time, I won't be so easy on you. That's a promise," Jim answered.

"Well, you're 0 for 1, but let's not talk about your I.Q.," Randy replied, grinning.

The Lieutenant returned, very angry. "Damn, media! Always interfering with government business!"

By that comment and the look on the Lieutenant's face, Randy knew the media was now all over the story and had given at least preliminary reports. But before the Lieutenant could say anything else, Randy said, "Yep. The world knows about all five CASPs, where and why we're here. Hell, your name might come up, too!"

Charlie added, "I know Jim's name will come up too, especially when his kitten-of-the-month calendar comes out."

Randy continued, "This covert mission you command has been completely compromised, and you're still taking us back. That won't look good to the promotion board. You know how it is when an Officer is given an order and fails to execute it. That doesn't show great leadership abilities. So, Lieutenant, my only question now is, when will lunch be served on the ship? Nothing extravagant, mind you. But I think we all could use some refreshments. You know, at least some finger food. Hey! Maybe a cheese platter with sliced fruit around the edge like kiwi and strawberries." He drew the image with his finger in the air. "You know, sometimes they put a few mint leaves on top. That's nice because the dark green accentuates and complements the lighter color of the cheeses, and the colorful fruit slices make a nice border. I enjoy a good visual presentation for my cheese platters. And I almost hate to take the first piece of cheese because it ruins it, but I do anyway." Randy winked at the angry-looking Lieutenant before turning to his brother and sister, Caspers, "Friends, take a last look!" He threw his hands in the air. "We're going home!" Cheers and clapping erupted from the overjoyed group.

The Lieutenant placed his hand on his holstered sidearm.

"Sure," Charlie said. "Add mass murder of civilians to the list of crimes. It will be on every one of these guys' helmet cams. That way, your name is guaranteed to be all over the news."

"You'll all be taken back to the ship in cuffs. Sergeant." The Lieutenant said with a deflated tone.

Charlie whistled for Bear. "Let's go, Bear!"

The Lieutenant said, "The dog isn't coming. My orders didn't include a dog. That's what you get for being a bunch of smartasses."

Charlie was close enough to punch the Lieutenant in the face. The Lieutenant went down, and Charlie immediately threw his hands up in surrender. "Okay! I'm cool. It's over!"

The sailor helped the Lieutenant up. "I ought to kick your ass right now! Put him in chains! The dog stays! The horses stay! And the damn chickens!" the Lieutenant shouted.

The soldiers emerged from the trees and entered the clearing. Williams and Monte approached Jim and the sailor. Williams said, "Pick up your weapons, remove the magazines, and clear them."

"And don't do anything stupid," Monte added. Jim and the Sailor did as they were told.

The two soldiers then walked over to Randy. Williams said, "We had your back, Dickensen. I told my men that we would not obey orders to shoot, and I would take the heat for it."

"I knew you wouldn't shoot. You two have always had my back."

Monte replied, "And you always had ours. What the hell are you doing here?"

"You guys remember that soul-science issue?"

"Yeah. That was some scary shit," Williams replied.

"The Army selected me to have it done on. Dr. Brown promised it would make me a better soldier."

Monte grinned. "Sounds like my bullshit recruiter."

"It screwed me all up at first. Dr. Brown hid us here so no one would know. We've been here for over a year."

Williams said, "Damn. So, this is what this big top-secret mission is about."

"But now you're going home. Brother, we'll catch up later." They shook hands.

The Caspers allowed themselves to be handcuffed and followed the stretcher carrying Dennis down the trail to the beach. Charlie walked in chains. The soldiers, still alarmed by the shooting and much more by the ring of life energy, kept their weapons ready as the seventeen Caspers made their way to the rubber rafts. Jim stood at the edge of the trail. Jim gave Randy a nasty look as the Caspers passed by and said, "There'll be another time, Randy."

"Nah, I don't think so, Igor. I don't often visit prisons. You'll always be 0 for 1."

"Why the hell do you keep calling me 'Igor'?

"You'll have a long time to think about that."

The Caspers were ushered onto the two rubber rafts waiting on the beach. As they pulled away, Bear stood watching and barking. All the Caspers watched in tears and anger as Bear's image and barking faded.

Charlie yelled over to the Lieutenant, "So help me, if we ever meet again, I'll personally kick the shit out of you! You better hope that I never see you again!"

The Lieutenant just gave an exaggerated smile.

On Their Way Home

On the Coast Guard ship, the Caspers were seated in the empty mess hall and ankle-cuffed to their chairs. Commercials on the muted television mounted on the wall momentarily took their attention. They hadn't seen a TV for a year.

Three Navy Officers and a woman in a business suit walked in as two armed soldiers stood near the walls.

"Hello. Which one of you is Randy?" the senior Officer asked.

"I'm Randy. Where's Dennis?"

"He's being taken care of in the infirmary. I just came from there. They tell me it's a wonder he's not cooling off in a body bag. Before

123

we arrive at the port, I'd like to ask some questions after introducing you to your lawyer."

The woman in the business suit introduced herself as their court-appointed lawyer. "Hello. My name is Tonya Murphy."

"Okay," Randy casually replied.

The officers and the lawyer pulled up chairs in front of Randy, who was excited about going home and couldn't help but be more playful.

"Sure. But we're still waiting for our refreshments, especially the cheese platter, as I described to the Lieutenant back on the island. It's been a long day. We can't think on an empty stomach, but we can talk while we eat."

The other Caspers didn't try to cover their chuckles.

The Officer looked frustrated. "Alright, I'll order sandwiches and coffee. He nodded to a subordinate Officer who left the room. Minutes later, several nervous-looking seamen entered the room with platters and served the Caspers.

As Randy enjoyed his sandwich, the senior Officer, growing impatient, began, "Randy, my first question is, how and where did you get that satellite system and the radio?"

"Let 'me begin with my first question," Randy said. "Why do we need a lawyer? Was there a crime committed? Have we been charged with anything?"

The lawyer answered, "There are no charges at this time. I'm your legal representative if you are charged with crimes."

Randy was ready to take another bite of his sandwich and replied, "All of you need to understand the context here. The government-paid scientists botched our A.S.P procedures, told our families and everyone else that we died, and hid us on an island against our wills, essentially destroying our lives, and it's 'us' who might be charged with crimes. Lady, you're a government lawyer, but even you must see the irony here. We're not talking to you or answering any questions from anyone at this point. And besides that, there's no cheese platter. Was that too much to ask for? And one more thing," He pointed at the senior Officer and then to his sandwich. "This bread is a little dry." He held his sandwich close to his eyes and rotated it for inspection. "I do like the mustard, though." He looked around at the other Caspers. "How are your sandwiches?" They all laughed and talked over one another, making remarks about the crispness of the lettuce, the kind of cheese, the flavor of the smoked turkey, the freshness of the tomatoes, and the temperature of the coffee. The frustrated Officers looked at each other, disappointed, and stood up with the lawyer to leave.

Scarlett noticed that the silent TV showed a breaking news report with their picture next to the announcer's head. "Hey, look, everyone! That's us!"

In closed captioning, the news anchorman said, "Continuing with the breaking news from yet an unknown source, it is alleged that nearly ninety damaged victims of the Advanced Soul Project, previously thought to have died, have been rescued from five secret islands after having been taken against their wills." A picture of Dr. Carol Brown appeared on the screen. The news anchorwoman beside him continued, "That's right, Dan. Without electricity or plumbing, these victims managed to survive for over a year. It's not known yet who blew the whistle. Still, these crimes were allegedly committed with the full knowledge and help of Dr. Carol Brown, director of the Advanced Soul Program, and at least three US senators named in the mysterious letter, and some members of the US military are also named in the letter."

The anchorman said, "Well, Mandy, you can bet there are some heavy investigations already in progress."

The anchorwoman replied, "As we get more clarity and developments, we'll pass them on to you. Stay right here."

All the Caspers cheered. The Officers and the lawyer left the noisy room.

Throughout the day, news anchors on TV were still interrupting regularly scheduled programs with the news that they were trying to confirm a report that nearly ninety victims of the infamous and failed Advanced Soul Project were still alive and were presently arriving back from their captivity from remote locations. The picture from the CASP community number 5 was displayed on the screen with every report.

Further reports included the names of the politicians who allegedly approved the program and the military officers who ordered the operation to be carried out.

'Margaret and Georgina,' Randy thought to himself and smiled. "Thanks for that extra touch."

The Coast Guard ship approached the dock, covered by a massive crowd of protesters and reporters from every media outlet gathered for the arrival. Georgina and her group ensured the public knew the 'who, what, where, when, why, and how.' Police cars with their lights on were parked all around, along with an ambulance. Several dark SUVs waited off to the side of the crowd. Pedestrian barriers were placed along the route that the Caspers would walk.

Eventually, three sailors came into the room to remove the ankle cuffs. "Please follow me," one of them said. He led the Caspers back through guarded hallways and bulkheads to the gangway, where they stopped and looked out at the large gathering. A surge of noise erupted from the crowd.

"Buses," Natasha noted. "I wonder why they're parked there."

"Yeah, but it doesn't matter. We're not getting on the bus. I wonder if the people in the buses were at least some of the other Caspers, if not all of them," Randy replied.

"I bet you're right," Natasha said.

The Navy Officer in front of them turned around to Randy. "Sir, we'll safely escort you to that bus and take you back to the hospital to be examined. Please have the group follow me."

He turned and took a few steps to lead the group. Randy didn't follow.

"You're not taking us to the government's laboratory, and we won't be examined. Let me tell you what's going to happen. We are taking a public transportation bus to follow the ambulance with Dennis to the public hospital."

The Officer turned around and walked back to threaten Randy. "Sir, I can have you arrested right here, right now. You will follow me to the bus and board it."

Randy leaned toward the Officer to look him in the eyes, challenging him. "You do that. Arrest me and all the others. Let the world watch as the government once again takes us against our will to a place we would have refused to go had we been given a choice, and then finally tells the nation that we died a second time. Do it while the TV cameras are rolling, and hundreds of people watch live, with your face being the one the world sees and remembers. The videos would travel around the world before we got to the other end of the gangway."

Theresa added, "I'm sure the government could use a little PR help just about now, and the trip to the public hospital on a public bus might make things look better."

Randy said, "One more thing. I'm riding in the ambulance with Dennis."

The Officer took his radio, stepped back, and spoke to someone Randy assumed was with the FBI. The Officer relayed Randy's terms.

"Okay," the Officer said after the radio conversation. "The city bus will be here in a few minutes, Sir. I'll escort you to the end of the gangway. From there, you'll be walked to the ambulance by state troopers. After that, I'll lead the others down the gangway. The troopers will see that they safely get on the public bus and are escorted to the public hospital."

Randy turned around to the group. "Friends, I'm going with Dennis. I'll see you all at the hospital. If there's any deviation from what we've agreed to, all of you fight like hell. Follow Charlie's lead. Sit close together on the bus so you can hold hands if needed. Give the world the kind of parade they've never seen before."

The Navy Officer walked Randy down the ship's brow, where Randy was handed off to two state troopers. The security barricades were lined with police to protect the three men from the thick walls of pressing demonstrators and aggressive media shouting questions at them. Randy smiled and waved but didn't stop or make a statement.

As the Caspers walked toward the city buses, intending to take them back to the ASP facility. Dr. Carol Brown stood at the front of the first bus with her arms folded and glared at the group. She was more than disappointed; she was angry and so focused on her test subjects parading in freedom in front of her that she didn't see the two U.S. Marshal agents walk up to her. They placed her in handcuffs, read her rights, and walked her to a dark sedan parked nearby.

When Randy arrived at the ambulance, he looked through the back doors and saw that Dennis was already lying inside. One of the state troopers opened the door for Randy. He climbed in to take a seat beside Dennis, opposite the attending doctor. The trooper climbed in to sit next to him. The other trooper closed the back doors and headed for his car to lead the way.

"Let's go," the doctor ordered the driver.

Two police cars with lights on escorted the ambulance. One car led in front of the ambulance, and the other followed closely behind it.

"How are you feeling, my friend?" Randy asked, placing his hand on his friend's hand.

"Better," Dennis answered. "Those doctors called me a 'miracle,' wondering how I survived. But I didn't bother explaining. The first bullet took a piece of bone off my femur, and the second bullet passed between two ribs. It didn't hit anything too important. I'm thankful that my life energy is high." He winked. "I'm so glad you're here, Randy."

"I wouldn't have it any other way. The rest of our group will be following us on a bus. Dennis, we're going to a public hospital, and you'll have surgery to get you back on your feet. We'll all be there the whole time you're there."

"Okay. Good."

The Hospital's security had noticeably increased. Uniformed police Officers and men and women in dark suits and sunglasses stood at the entrance to the hospital, dotted the parking lots, and guarded the doors. The Caspers exited the bus and were escorted to a secure waiting room, where Dr. Morgan was waiting to surprise them.

As he waited for the Caspers, it was evident to Dr. Morgan that the only other person in the room, a clean-shaven guy with a 'high-and-tight' haircut, was pretending to be a visitor. It seemed the FBI agent was hastily ordered to the room, so he didn't have time to find his size of casual shoes, so he had to wear the nice shoes he wore to work that morning. The perfect black polished shoes, the college ring, and the expensive watch seemed out of place alongside the dirty, ripped jeans and an undersized, wrinkled flannel shirt. And his worn hat didn't look natural on him. The 'average Joe' doesn't usually cross his legs at the knees. Further, the visitor chose the science magazine over the hunting magazine on the side table. None of these would make anyone suspicious, but the man didn't pass the smell test when they were together. Dr. Morgan didn't want him there when the Caspers arrived.

"Nice shoes."

"Pardon?" The man's educated language confirmed that he was out of character. Dr. Morgan decided that the question, "What?" would have been expected as a response from an average person in this informal setting.

"Your shoes. They're nice."

"Thank you," the Agent replied. A more common reply, 'Thanks,' wasn't offered. Neither was an explanation for the mismatched ensemble.

"Visiting someone?" the Doctor continued in a friendly tone.

"Yes," the man smiled. My wife is having a baby." The Doctor observed the absence of a wedding ring, which was another clue to the agent's masquerade.

"Well, Agent, you're on the wrong wing and floor. Women typically give birth to their babies on the second floor of the north wing. Additionally, FBI agents are typically better prepared for these undercover activities. They rushed you here, didn't they? You screeched into the parking lot of a convenience store to buy cigarettes, raced your car to the hospital, abruptly parked in the first space you saw, sprinted through the halls flashing your badge to a couple of people, dashed up the stairs, and did your best to catch your breath before I got here. And here you sit, hoping I wouldn't notice all the inconsistencies in your appearance."

The agent looked at the doctor with a glimmer of surprise, placed his magazine over the pack of cigarettes on the table, and stood.

"I don't know what you're talking about, but I should have looked at the directory more closely. I'd better get going. I need to check on my wife!"

"Good idea. You do that. And congratulations on your newborn, fake story."

After the man left the room, Dr. Morgan shook his head, reaching over to take the cigarettes from under the magazine. He opened the pack to discover three missing cigarettes, and a listening device filled the space. While he was enjoying his cup of coffee, he was even more satisfied when he dropped the bug into his coffee. "Amateur."

Moments later, Randy walked in. His armed escort waited outside the door. The two men stood smiling and hugged, knowing their conversation could be overheard.

"You made it!" Dr. Morgan declared.

"Yes, I did. We all did. Not exactly in one piece, though. Dennis took a couple of rounds from Jim's itchy trigger finger. He should be in surgery by now."

"So, I heard. Dennis is in surgery now. I'll stop in and check on him again, but he should be fine. Now, what's next for you and the others?"

Randy replied, "From the beginning, all we ever wanted was to go home. Dr. Morgan, we want to go home, be reunited with our families, and try to live normal lives again. That's not asking much."

Dr. Morgan replied, "Especially after all you've been through. The politicians, Dr. Brown, and the other A.S.P directors will be preoccupied with investigations, hearings, and lawsuits. But eventually, they're going to want to see all of you."

"I agree they will, but it's up to each one of us if, how much, and when."

"Randy, as you might know, I've written several books. Someday, you and I should collaborate on writing one. It would be a very intriguing story that everyone will want to read."

"I like that proposition."

Moments later, the other Caspers, busy in conversations, could be heard coming down the hall. After they walked through the door, they exchanged hugs, handshakes, and big smiles with Dr. Morgan.

After the successful surgery, Dennis spent just two days recovering before being released. His friends had gone into his room and held hands around his bed. The life energy sped up his healing and recovery.

On the day of Dennis's release, Dr. Morgan visited the Caspers at the hospital. "The government wants to help all of you restart your lives by giving you some money. You might call it a guilt offering with the attempt to pacify you." He handed out thick envelopes to the Caspers gathered around. "There is fifty thousand dollars in cash in each envelope. It should be enough to get you back on track in society. There are also some IDs and debit cards to help you get airline reservations or rent a car for your trips home." A guard handed Dr. Morgan a box. The doctor opened it, saying, "Here are some cell phones. With each phone is a list of your names and numbers so you can stay in touch. My phone number is also listed there too. I don't need to remind you that we'll be listened to. I recommend keeping in touch at least every other day. Please let me know if you are unable to contact someone after two days. I'll personally follow up on it."

After they spoke, they decided not to wait any longer to return to their families and homes and promised to stay in touch with one another. They all hugged, and some cried. Randy took Natasha aside as they dispersed and shared his feelings about her.

"Natasha, I hope I managed to conceal my feelings toward you while we were on the island. As the leader, I had to. But now that we're back, I must tell you that I like you very much and hope it's mutual. I didn't have anyone before the CASP. I don't think you did either because you never talked about anyone special."

Natasha smiled. "I sensed you liked me, and the feelings are mutual, Randy. And you're right; I don't have anyone special either."

"Then, how about you and I start our new lives together? My folks have a nice finished basement with a couple of spare bedrooms. After you visit your family, you can come to live with us if you want, at least until we decide where we go from there."

"I'd like that, Randy," she said as she hugged him.

The LA Report published the exclusive story on the Caspers, purposely leaving out certain things and generalizing others. Margaret's loyalty to Randy protected him from further unnecessary questions and concealed some of his crimes that didn't have to be included. But the result was that the story was told.

The FBI meets the Bulldog.

As expected, Margaret was contacted by the FBI, who requested a meeting with her in her office. She agreed. Most other editors would be nervous, but Margaret played in the big league and often was the one who made the FBI nervous.

Before the Deputy Director arrived, Margaret took out one of the many old boxes she kept in the back of the bottom shelf of her cabinet. After searching them, she placed a box on her desk, opened it, and carefully took out three framed headline articles of big-name convictions that her newspaper had covered, convictions that came in part due to her staff's investigative reporting. She hung them on the wall where the new Deputy Director would have to notice them, and she knew they would serve as a notice that this Bulldog might not bark before it bit.

Margaret invited Deputy Director Thomas to sit in the chair on the other side of the little table. Margaret had arranged the furniture to be in the middle of her office, with the back of the Deputy Director's chair facing the office door. Her guest was a middle-aged, plain-looking woman in a plain business suit. Margaret sat in the other chair across from a little table. Just before they began to talk, the young man from Georgina's office knocked on the door while balancing a tray of coffee cups, cream, sugar, and water bottles.

"Come in," Margaret said.

The young man from Georgina's office entered with the tray, walked past the guest, and placed each item on the little table between the seated women.

"Excuse me. Here you go, ladies." He walked away with the empty tray.

"How nice. Thank you," the Deputy Director said.

"Oh, you're very welcome," the young man replied as he turned and returned to the door. Just before he left, he looked down at a small device in his hand, nodded to Margaret, and closed the door. The nod was the sign that the device he held under the tray had signaled the presence of an electronic listening device. Since Margaret frequently had her office electronically swept for bugs, she knew she had an attentive and extensive listening audience, and the Deputy Director held the secret microphone.

The Deputy Director looked around the office and picked up her cup of coffee. "Wow. So here I am at the LA Report and seated in the office with Margaret Stedman herself." She looked up at the framed articles on the wall. "You've helped topple a few big names over the years."

"I just exposed them. They toppled after that—just a few samples. I alternate them every so often. Sometimes, I put all of them up. It's rewarding to reminisce about my years of investigating and reporting." Margaret took a sip from her cup.

"I'm impressed with all the awards over on the other wall. You have them everywhere on shelves and walls. Which one are you most proud of?"

"My bronze bulldog," Margaret answered. "It has a special place on my desk. It's been there for a long time."

"Ms. Stedman, we have questions revolving around the escape and return of the leader of the Caspers from number 5. We believe Randy got a lot of outside help. You're a very well-connected person. Do you happen to know anything we should be aware of? Have you heard anything at all?"

"If I did know anything, I would have put it in the article to make it more interesting," Margaret replied. "It's what we do. You've heard the saying, 'If it bleeds, it leads.'"

"However, you did have the exclusive interview with Randy," the Deputy Director said.

"Yes. We have a mutual friend in Dr. Morgan. And since Sydney trusts me, Randy did as well."

"Alright. We're still digging. We got a few leads we're still following. One of them seems to point back here," the Deputy Director said with raised eyebrows.

"I'll call your bluff. Nothing leads back here unless you create it. Isn't it a mystery that one part of the government can fabricate evidence, and another part of the government can use it to prosecute someone? Exposing fabrications and their sources has been one of my favorite things. Some people seem to think I'm pretty good at it."

"Ms. Stedman, you must know the consequences of being involved with a crime. So, if there's anything at all that you need to tell me, now is the time."

"Director Deputy, allow me to be frank here. Ah, hell, I've never needed permission to speak my mind. Lady, you do your job. But keep in mind that the government is under tremendous pressure from the public, demanding that heads roll for the lies and destroyed lives of some of their fellow citizens. I don't know if the FBI has any sense of trepidation, but if they don't, they should because it's another disaster, and some of you might face prison. The government has pushing and pressuring folks in this investigation is hypocritical and arrogant. And you sit here trying to find anyone who might have committed a crime? Well, yes, some people have. And the FBI might once again be on that list. You must turn inward and see that proverbial beam in your eye. Believe me when I say that hypocrisy is a subject I will write about daily, especially when those in power are involved. If you need more bad PR, I'll gladly volunteer to be your nightmare. I'm very good at keeping people awake at night. Can you understand what I mean? You in the FBI don't want to start pushing me around again. It didn't go well for the last person who tried. You've got your own house to get in order, and I've got a lot more space on my walls that I'd like to fill before I retire." She pointed to the wall. "Filling every space on that wall is one of the last things on my bucket list, and I would very much like to draw a line through that goal before I leave. Of course, I can stay on longer if I need to. It depends on how long the trials go. I'm glad our little talk is being broadcast to the bureau; that way, we don't have to have this conversation again."

The Deputy Director looked at Margaret, wondering if she knew she had a wire, was assuming she did, or was just being paranoid. She decided to call her out.

"Being 'broadcasted,' Ms. Stedman?"

"C'mon, Ms. Thomas. I've been playing this game long before you stood on the sidewalk looking up in awe at the building, ready to begin your first day at the FBI Academy. And I've gotten damn good at the game over the years. Your wire set a silent alarm, confirming how predictable you people are. While I'm aware of the wire, I have an educated guess that there's also a micro-camera in your necklace or one disguised as a button on your jacket. And while I have nothing to hide, the camera's video signal is being electronically scrambled as we sit here enjoying our coffee."

"Yes, I believe I do understand you." The Deputy Director generally maintained a controlled demeanor. "Thank you for your time. Let me say this with respect, Ms. Stedman. I see how you got your reputation and the bronze Bulldog on your desk. The real-life Margaret Stedman is larger than even the legend." She glanced at the frames on the wall before she stood and walked toward the door. "Thank you for the coffee."

After the Deputy Director left, Georgina came up to Margaret's office. "Well, how do you think it went?"

"Well, if someone my age can use a phrase from a younger generation, I believe I 'ripped her a new one.'"

Dr. Morgan is called to testify.

In the meantime, Dr. Morgan's meeting with the jaded government officials and the embarrassed A.S.P board was also tense. Toward the end of the meeting, Dr. Brown had her time to grill Dr. Morgan. He opposed her with finesse as she sat sanctimoniously behind her microphone with the rest of the new committee at a long table elevated a little higher than the table at which Dr. Morgan sat alone.

"Thank you for coming to Dr. Morgan. Let's get directly to Casp number five. How is it that while under your supervision, one of the Caspers could escape, travel freely throughout California and wherever else, and return to the island, all without your knowledge?"

Dr. Morgan calmly replied, "Well, Dr. Brown, before I answer, let me congratulate you on your record time out of prison."

"Just answer the questions, please," Dr. Brown said, looking embarrassed.

"For one thing, I was on that island for just a few hours a month and surrounded by my team members. Questions concerning the security of that island and its occupants should be directed at those whose job it was to secure them. That sounds simple to me and probably to everyone else sitting here. But I understand your question. For a person living on a remote island, monitored and without electricity or any other modern conveniences, escaping undetected and returning in the same manner with some brand-new stolen military equipment is a feat of exceptional skill, surpassing even the escape from Alcatraz. The other half of my answer is this: Randy was successful in part because you and your team provided him with the means to be brilliant enough to plan, adapt, and evade despite your bumbling attempts to upgrade his soul. I'm surprised it took him a whole year to escape. I'm also surprised at the arrogance of this kind of question. You're looking for a scapegoat to redirect attention to. It's a common and obvious maneuver the guilty use to deflect responsibility. And you think I'm that person? No, Dr. Brown and ladies and gentlemen. The guilty ones will be seen the next time you look into your bathroom mirrors—those in the government and those in the

136

government's A.S.P program in the spotlight. And your respective criminal trials might finally give the government the wisdom to stop these soul manipulations, although I doubt it. It's no secret that I have spent many years opposed to it. Have you noticed yet that after every step of this soul-meddling, there were tragic consequences, not to mention another huge government embarrassment, long trials, convictions, and prison terms? And you ask me to sit in this chair to invite me to be your fall guy and question me as if I'm on trial? That's not going to happen. I'm not your fall guy. You broke it. Now you'll have to pay for it. God knows you can't fix it. Dr. Brown, ladies and gentlemen, how Randy got off the island is a minuscule issue. That there was such an island should be the focus. The fact that I refer to nearly a hundred failed test results as 'people' is also part of the focus. Nothing personal, but the next chair like this one that I sit in will be a witness chair at your trials because you still don't know when or where to stop."

Dr. Morgan stood from his chair.

Dr. Brown saw that he was ready to leave. "Dr. Morgan, there are a few other questions."

"Ladies and gentlemen, such is the extent of my knowledge, expert testimony, patience, and time. Thank you. I'm leaving now." He walked out of the meeting with dignity as surprised eyes followed him out the door.

Eventually, the government connected most of the dots regarding Randy's travels to and from the island. As Randy predicted, the hidden military car was discovered and reported by hunters. The buried uniform and tools were never found. The car's VIN and the serial numbers of the satellite system and radio led investigators to the military storage facility where the unsuspecting Corporal was interviewed. He finally told the story of the 'surprise inspection' by the Lieutenant. However, he did identify Randy through a picture. The Corporal wasn't disciplined because the imposter looked and behaved like an officer, and his story seemed plausible. The only rebuke was that the Corporal didn't know the Lieutenant's name. Randy kept the strap from his bag, covering where his name should have been. Both the Corporal and Randy knew it was not recommended for enlisted men to ask questions of Officers, especially when the Officer was irritated after having spent the night sitting in a dark car. As for the other stolen military radio, it was cleaned of any components that might receive or send a signal and featured in Georgina's secret group as her show-and-tell item. It was voted 'biggest win' of the month. All of them were happy to share credit for hacking into some government and military computers with their strategy of 'hacking their space and leaving no trace.'

Military investigators inspected Cargo Crate number 5. Blame was exchanged for the narrow, unreported compartment inside above the door. The craftsmanship and color made the long compartment look like an intentional addition, a necessary upgrade to the crate. Some warehouse workers concluded it was a great idea for smaller, fragile items.

Local authorities confirmed that the scuba gear was stolen from a small shop. Those items were never recovered. That equipment is buried deep in a hole on CASP number 5.

The 'accidental' and brief trespass into the restricted no-fly zone by a small aircraft near the island was never officially recorded and subsequently forgotten because the person on duty who gave the warning was also monitoring another frequency regarding a lost helium balloon school project. As hoped, the two seemingly unrelated events were never linked, and the incident was dismissed.

Randy and Natasha married six months after returning to the mainland. They invited Dr. and Mrs. Morgan, Margaret Stedman, and all the other Caspers from Island 5. The wedding allowed them to reconnect and exchange updates and stories about being casually contacted by friendly government officials concerning their abilities and progress. Of course, in those times, the Caspers were not very compliant. They didn't have to be. Although they were surprised at how easily they were allowed to melt back into their everyday lives, even the ominous absence of interference from the government bred a mild 'look-behind-you' suspicion.

The other Caspers, from 1 to 4, had also re-entered society, finding new lives or reconnecting with their past. They, too, were surprised by the government's apparent 'hands-off' attitude. Each of their leaders contacted Randy. Everyone agreed to have a secret annual Casper reunion.

Natasha bought an orchard with greenhouses and ran a successful business, utilizing her extraordinary powers on her plants. She was frequently asked about the type of fertilizer she used that caused her trees and plants to grow as they did. "Lots and lots of love," she told them.

Sharon took on two full-time jobs because she had to sleep only one day a week.

Theresa opened her own business playing music for hypnotic therapy and relaxation. Her gift was in demand from people all over the world. Clients will travel great distances after scheduling an hour to lie on their couch in a dim, private room with incense. Her music gracefully invaded the client's minds and souls, bringing them to depths of relaxation, peace, and perspective they couldn't have experienced by any other means. She rarely accepted invitations to travel worldwide to give her therapy to wealthy clients.

Lily earned a substantial income working as an international translator for businesses and governments. She was one of only two people in the world who could easily speak and accurately translate a dozen languages simultaneously. The only other person who could do this was Casper from CASP 3.

Olivia taught advanced electrical engineering at a college without a degree, but she's working on it.

Charlie traveled around teaching his course, 'Basic Living Techniques and Practices,' to like-minded communes and communities. He met a student, Maria, and they ended up getting married.

Dennis was a main attraction at zoos everywhere due to his ability to draw and connect with animals in captivity and the wild. He was featured on the news after being filmed walking up to a pride of lions at a game reserve and sitting down with them. The lions immediately adopted him into the pride.

The Caspers, who became ill and suffered from the experiments, tried to find ways to cope. Charges were never brought against Randy. There would have been a massive protest if the government had attempted to do so. Randy was placed on probation for a year and had to check in once a month to make the federal prosecutor feel like he at least tried to do his job. Furthermore, Randy was offered the opportunity to teach courses at the CIA academy due to his brilliance in every step of his escape. He didn't teach them everything he knew, but he made an impression nonetheless. The other Caspers from CASP 5 had easily returned to society. Like all the others, they found places for their unique abilities while trying to manage their impediments.

Every other Casp had tried to duplicate the Caspers' ring, but it proved futile. Nature required an exact combination of specific components to manifest its life energy in the powerful way it did. It might be less challenging to discover what the extracted parts of the donor souls were. Even more difficult would be to understand and copy the mistakes in the ASP process.

Nova – Nature's Stepchild

Ten months after Randy and Natasha got married, they had a baby, an extraordinary baby girl who, even at six months old, could walk and speak basic sentences. To say that Nova was incredible is an understatement. To say that she was astonishing was getting closer to the truth. Sometimes, she would sit by herself and hum. The hum was the same tone from her mother's garden back on the island and the same tone from the ring of life energy that surrounded Dennis twice. But it wasn't just a tone with Nova. There was also a new and unique vibration.

Her parents chose to homeschool Nova partially to limit her exposure to the world and partly because, by the age of one, she could already read at a seventh-grade level and had a basic understanding of math. She absorbed information and mastered it at an astonishing rate.

When Randy and Natasha took Nova to her pediatrician, they asked her to pretend she couldn't speak and act like a normal child of her age. Nova was intelligent enough to play the proper part. During the times when a teacher from the school district visited to test her skills, Nova deceitfully displayed a level of skills just above her age, although she was years ahead. When her mother took her shopping, she could not speak to adoring customers like she could. She mimicked language skills that would be normal for a child her age. Nova enjoyed playing these pretend games and understood why she had to do so.

Early one morning, while it was still dark, Natasha got out of bed and walked to the kitchen to make coffee before she went to work. She wasn't surprised to hear her ten-year-old daughter sitting alone in silence on the carpet in the living room with her eyes closed, humming the tune. Nova often did this. But at that moment, Natasha looked over at her daughter and suddenly stopped, staring at her. Natasha saw a faint light-blue hue enveloping Nova in the room's darkness. She walked silently closer to her daughter to observe thousands and thousands of tiny strands of multiple colors swimming freely within the blue hue. Nova spread her hands in front of her, and the life energy formed a flare between them. Natasha quietly stepped back, continued to the kitchen, and cried, but she didn't know why.

Later that night, Natasha shared the incident with Randy. "I think the energy is growing in her, and she's learning to control it."

"Maybe. If our daughter does learn, who knows the limits to what she could do?"

Such will be Nova's private life until she can't be hidden anymore. Her parents feared that day, and so did Dr. Morgan. Even though he and his wife had excitedly agreed to be Nova's godparents, they were among the few who knew of her specialness. Privately, Dr. Morgan was very concerned about what Nova might become. Sometimes at night, he lay in the dark, thinking that Nova was potentially the sweetest and cutest slow-motion disaster ever waiting to impact the world. However, his biggest fear was that she might be similar to the Genetically Improved Soul or G.I.S., which he had warned the Senate about years ago. He feared that could be her future. The difference is that it was 'nature' that constructed the components of her soul at conception and not a machine in a laboratory. Who knew if the world was prepared for Nova, whose soul was already equipped with magnified abilities? Her conception naturally combined the intellectual brilliance of one parent with special powers and a natural affinity for nature from the other, along with a very high level of natural life energy. The inevitable introduction of Nova Dickensen to the world approached quickly.

The Zoo

Randy, Natasha, and Nova had invited Dr. Morgan and his wife to spend the day at the zoo. The Morgans were elderly now and usually walked slower than everyone except when fourteen-year-old Nova walked between her 'Papa' and 'Mema' holding their hands. Her life energy had often helped them over the past years. The effects of Mrs. Morgan's devastating stroke had become minimal. Dr. Morgan seemed to be winning his battle with the sudden discovery of his stage-three cancer, even without radiation treatments and chemotherapy. Statistically speaking, he should have died by now, and his wife should at least be in an assisted living facility or hospice. However, today, they both walked briskly around the zoo.

The group didn't stay long at any exhibit because the combined life energy from Randy, Natasha, and Nova quickly got the animals' attention, and they often moved toward them. The giraffes turned and started to walk over. Elephants trumpeted toward them. A silverback gorilla picked up a ball and rolled it toward the window as if inviting the five spectators to play. A large male lion who often ignored the zoo visitors trotted to the viewing window and lay on his back, waiting for his belly to be rubbed. After a brief look at the animals up close and a few quick pictures, it was time for the small group to move on to the next exhibit before anyone could connect them to the uncanny behaviors of the animals.

The Gray Wolf exhibit was another crowded attraction, with numerous people trying to peer down into the natural-looking habitat. Parents with strollers and visitors with cameras squeezed their way to the rail, trying to take their turns to look down at the pack of eight wolves fifteen feet below. The wolves appeared to be accustomed to this and no longer looked up at the daily commotion of spectators, except when someone broke the posted rules and threw a piece of French fries at them or a piece of a hot dog. Unfortunately, today was one of those times.

At first, no one noticed the man kneeling at the rail. He pushed himself out over the rail and reached down to offer his half-eaten hamburger to the wolves. As expected, the wolves took notice and approached the offer. They circled and waited for the little meal to be dropped. Suddenly, one of the wolves crouched and sprang up, using the nails on its back feet to get traction on the wall. Then, he grabbed the man by his wrist. The weight of the dangling wolf was enough to pull the man down into the pit. As he landed with a crash, the air in the man's lungs billowed with a loud gush. Moaning, he backed himself against the wall and sat still. The wolves snarled and bared long fangs that snapped at him. They were ready to go in for the kill.

In the screams and commotion, Nova went through the spectators and slipped unnoticed to the other side of the exhibit. She took hold of a vine growing around a tree at the pit's edge. It was apparent that she didn't climb down the vine, which appeared to grow rapidly, letting her down into the exhibit. When the spectators saw Nova, some screamed and pointed, while others recorded the event on their cell phones and cameras. They all understood that none could help the girl or the man already sitting terrified in the pit.

The crouching wolves lunged at the man, biting his feet and tugging at his pant legs as he kicked at them with his other foot. The bottoms of his pants were shredded, one of his shoes was ripped, and his socks were stained with blood. Two of the wolves wrestled over the other shoe that they had yanked off his foot in an attempt to drag the man into the center of the pit.

Instantly, the wolves stopped their attack, dropped the shoe, and turned to look at the young, defenseless-looking teenage girl who walked toward them from the other side of the pit. She was humming, but no one could hear it above the commotion. Her parents just watched and pretended to be concerned. They knew she wasn't in danger. The wolves started wagging their tails as she got nearer. They went over to meet her, yelping with joy as if they were puppies, and Nova was their mother who had just returned after a long absence. Licking her hands and chin, they whined as she freely petted them. Nova's parents just shook their heads in between insincere shouts of panic. Natasha turned to Randy and spoke in his ear, "And so it begins."

The caretaker's door inside the exhibit opened, and three employees with guns slowly and cautiously stepped out into the pit.

"I'm okay. You can help the man over there. He's hurt," Nova calmly said.

But the three rescuers continued to walk directly toward her and the pack of wolves.

"Young lady, don't move!" They ordered. The wolves all moved before her to bark and growl warnings at the approaching trio.

"I'm fine! Help him!" She pointed to the bleeding man sitting in pain below the spectators. "You can take the man to the hospital. Go ahead! The wolves won't hurt anyone while I'm here."

The confused employees turned and moved cautiously toward the terrified man, who managed his best to remain very still in his agony, sat against the wall, trembling, and held his bleeding arm while trying to catch his breath.

"Sir, can you walk?!"

"Yes. I think so. But barely and just on one leg. Get me out of here, please!"

Wincing in pain, the rescuers assisted the man, who helped him by placing his arms over their shoulders and supporting him back to the door. The third rescuer walked backward, watching the wolves, who happily turned their attention back to Nova.

Nova told the wolves, "Okay. I have to go now. I'll try to come back and visit you." She walked to the door, and the wolves followed, still wagging their tails. As she arrived at the door, Nova turned and looked at them and said, "You be good." She knelt face to face and pointed her finger at them. "And no more junk food! It's not good for you."

The wolves licked her fingers, then yelped in protest and howled and cried, obviously saddened by her leaving as one of the rescuers pulled her in the door.

The videos and pictures from the spectators went super-viral. The media dubbed her "The Wolf Girl." Other than the apparent mysteries of how a girl survived and seemed to communicate with the wolves, there was another anomaly in the videos - the vine growing rapidly as she held onto it and let her down into the pit. The good news was that because of the noise from the spectators and the wolves, no one heard the low hum coming from the vine, and the bright daylight concealed enough of the blue hue of life energy around her.

Of course, the government eventually saw the internet videos. They contacted Randy and Natasha, asking if they would allow Nova to be examined by their experts. Her parents refused, and the government was disappointed. Some seemed not to want to take 'no' for an answer. Dr. Brown was still one of them.

Botched Abduction

Coincidentally or not, one day shortly after the event at the zoo, as Natasha and Nova were walking down the sidewalk, a white van approached from behind and screeched to a stop. Two men jumped out of the sliding door, pushed Natasha to the ground, and whisked Nova into the van. Natasha screamed and watched the van rapidly start to pull away. She ran after the van, watching in terror until the brake lights came on, and the van slowed down to bump gently into a telephone pole. The sliding door opened. Nova stepped out and ran back to her mother. A few other pedestrians ran up to the van to apprehend the assailants. Pulling the passenger door open, they yelled to Natasha, "They're knocked out like sleeping or something! But they're moaning a little!

"Honey, let's go." Natasha took Nova's hand. They quickly walked away before the police arrived.

Finding a small ice cream store, they sat inside and watched as police cars with sirens and lights sped by. Natasha's voice was calm. "Nova, what happened in the van? They didn't hurt you, did they?"

"No, Mom. I took some life energy from the two men holding me, making them sleepy. They fell over. Then I stood and put my hand on the driver's shoulder, and he closed his eyes and slumped against his door window. I pushed the brake pedal and steered the van to bump the pole so I could get out. Steering the van was the only scary part. I just about had to sit on the guy's lap. Eeew!"

"That was very brave and smart, honey. I'm glad you're safe. Were you afraid?"

"No. Not really. But mom, you're talking to me like I'm a normal fifteen-year-old."

"Natasha looked confused. "Well, you are fifteen, and you appear to be fourteen. Sometimes, I look at you and forget you're exceptional and well beyond your age."

Nova stared at her dish of ice cream and then looked up at her mom, tears welling up in her eyes. "Mom… do you ever wish I were a normal teenage girl?" Tears trickled down her face. "If I were you, Daddy wouldn't have to worry and pretend so much."

"Nooo, honey." Natasha reached over and held her daughter's face in her hands. "You're my daughter and your daddy's daughter. What you are and what you have are from us." Natasha brought her smiling face close to Nova and widened her eyes in response. "What we are is a very abnormal little family of misfits." They both laughed and continued to enjoy their ice cream.

"Mom, I could have pulled all the life out of them while never touching them. I'm only telling you that because I don't want you to worry about me. I'm not fragile or vulnerable. Those men were not the predators they thought they were, and I will never be the prey. I'll use whatever power I must to protect myself and others."

146

"I'm so glad to hear that, Nova. I am. So now there's only one thing left to do."

"What's that, Mom?"

"We must figure out what type of superhero costumes we must wear. Maybe a cape and a mask for each one of us. Or, we can get two of those impractical but hot, sexy black plastic outfits that some other female superheroes wear! You know, the ones - tight and shiny. We won't be able to move in them very well, and we will sweat a lot. We won't be able to run very fast in the matching high-heel lace-up boots, but we'll look fabulous as we casually walk away from a big explosion behind us. Oh! And we can crack our necks! You see those things in so many movies now. We should stroll, placing one foot in front of the other like walking down a model's runway in a fashion show!" Natasha threw her hands up. "Can you imagine how fabulous we'd look?!"

Nova laughed at her mom's wide eyes and expressive gestures and gently pushed her shoulder. "Mom! Stop. That's ridiculous. I'll stick to jeans and blouses. But I do want a pair of those boots!"

Other incidents occurred sporadically over the next few months as Nova learned to channel, increase, and control life energy. Thankfully, for her sake, most of these powerful exhibits of life energy were kept from the public's knowledge.

Hidden from the media was the time she suddenly came upon a mugging in progress, where she again took life energy from the muggers by simply extending her hand toward them. The muggers dropped to their knees before falling to the ground, unconscious. In the commotion, neither the muggers nor the victim noticed her peeking into the alley from around the corner of the building. Also, the public didn't know when the canoe overturned on the lake. The two teenagers in the water apparently couldn't swim and had no life jackets. They floundered in the water, choking, splashing, and in the process of drowning as they tried in vain to reach the canoe and the life jackets that were just pushed away by their splashing arms. Nova was passing by the lake and heard the cries for help. She jumped off her bicycle and ran to the edge of the lake. Kneeling in the mud at the lake's edge, she put her hand in the water and began to hum. Just below the surface of the water, her hand turned light blue. The blue energy spread over the water's surface, looking like a thin, light-blue layer of morning fog. The reeds and lily pads near the shore trembled. Frogs kept jumping high into the air, and fish of every size in the area were attracted and directed to form a tight splashing mass under the drowning victims. The fish pushed up under the two teens. The water sizzled beneath the two boys as the fish kept them buoyant on the water's surface, forcing them into shallow water. When the terrified teens felt the bottom of the lake with their feet, they crawled up to the shore. Nova pulled her hand out of the water. The lake and its inhabitants returned to normal, and the fish dispersed. Once Nova determined the two teens would be fine, she returned to her bicycle and pedaled away. The two boys went home and told the story to their parents, who suspected that the boys were bored and had made most of their story up to create a bit of excitement and distract from the fact that they weren't wearing their life jackets.

Death for a Mile Around

Traffic flowed on the freeway as Dr. Morgan drove along, enjoying the morning. His wife, Ellen, who sat beside him, was slightly turned to the left in conversation with Randy, Natasha, and Nova, who sat tightly together in the back seat. The group was going to a restaurant to celebrate Nova's sixteenth birthday. She proudly wore the beautiful new necklace the Morgans had bought her.

Dr. Morgan stayed in the conversation by frequently looking up and talking with his friends through the rear-view mirror, sometimes adjusting his view to watch the person speaking. Occasionally, he would swerve a little to get back in the center of his lane. Randy noticed the danger in Dr. Morgan's distraction and struggled to think of what to say and how to say it because the Morgans were dear friends.

"Papa Sydney, why don't you and I change places so you can sit back by the birthday girl? I don't mind taking a turn at the wheel."

Dr. Morgan looked up to answer while again adjusting his mirror, providing a few moments of dangerous inattention. He didn't see the red brake lights come on from the big truck in front of him.

"Papa! Watch out!" Nova screamed. Dr. Morgan looked down from the rear-view mirror but didn't have time even to apply the brakes. He managed a slight turn but still hit the edge of the big truck's bumper. The car's hood crumpled as the airbags deployed and the windshield shattered. Everyone yelled and screamed. The impact sent the car skidding and spinning off the side of the road, where the car rolled multiple times, ejecting Mrs. Morgan before landing hard on its tires in a cloud of dirt and dust. The passengers in the rear seat were dazed, but after a few moments, they managed to get out and help. Randy threw dirt on the small flame near the engine. The driver's side door wouldn't open, so Randy reached through the broken window, unbuckled the unconscious doctor, and pulled him out of the car through the window. Together, Randy and Natasha supported the doctor under his arms and dragged him over near his dirty wife, who was lying still, a safe distance away from the wrecked smoking car. Mrs. Morgan's bleeding head was twisted around too far. Her eyes were half-opened. Natasha checked in vain for a pulse that reluctantly confirmed that Mrs. Morgan was dead, but didn't say it aloud. Nova's mind finally took in the carnage, and she began to cry with profound sorrow that only someone who had lost a person they dearly loved would know.

Dr. Morgan struggled to speak faintly between labored breaths and slow words. "Ellen? How is Ellen?" He found enough strength to roll his head toward his wife. He saw her tranquil face. "She's dead, isn't she?"

"Yes. I'm so sorry," Natasha admitted, sobbing.

Nova dropped to her knees with both hands over her face, screaming, "Mema! No!"

Moments later, Dr. Morgan succumbed to his injuries. By the looks on her parents' faces, Nova realized that both her Papa and Mema were dead. Sobbing, she ran and knelt in between them, placing a hand on each of their heads.

"Honey, there's nothing that can be done now," her dad said with grief in his fatherly, gentle voice.

Nova stood to her feet, looked at the sky, clenched her hands into fists, and shrieked. But it was not only the sound of deep human sorrow; there was something else in her voice – a vibration. Even in the daylight, the familiar light-blue hue could be seen, forming and growing to envelop her entire body. Staring straight ahead in concentration while tears ran down her cheeks, she began to hum between gasps of sorrow. Suddenly, the same loud hum seemed to be coming from everywhere. Light-blue flares reached down from her hands to the unresponsive dead bodies at her sides. Randy and Natasha took a few more steps back and held hands. They hoped Nova could bring the Morgans back to life, but doubted she could. As the energy continued to grow, Randy and Natasha began to sense danger.

Natasha raised her voice, "Nova! They're gone. There's nothing you can do! Honey. Come on, we must let them go! I don't think you can control this!"

"Baby, you can't raise the dead! Come over here with us," her father called to her. Nova ignored them both. Maybe she couldn't hear them.

The intensity of the life energy grew. The light-blue energy turned dark blue. A massive, light-blue ring and dome formed over the entire area, turning the penetrating sunlight blue as Nova summoned life energy around her and gathered it from the ground, which trembled beneath her. She called all the life energy from the trees, which began to shiver. Birds flying in the area fell from the sky as she called in their life energy.

"Nova!" Natasha yelled. "It's too much! You can't handle it! Stop!"

Again, her mother's warning went unheeded. The glow around her grew as she channeled all the energy she could. Robbing nature itself of its life, she drew the life energy of everything she could, trying to give back life to the two dead loved ones lying there at her feet. The fragments of colors inside the dark blue hue swam faster in erratic patterns. It was as if life itself was being overcharged. Short flares thrust themselves out from the super-concentrated energy. Onlookers and good Samaritans gathered at the edge of the median to watch and try to help, but they feared that the vehicle had cut into an underground high-voltage cable, so they kept a safe distance.

Natasha's body became translucent and colorful, filled with millions of tiny swimming strands of multiple colors. Up high from the center of the dome, a long flare reached down and slowly lifted Nova. Her parents embraced each other as their eyes followed her up. She rose several yards off the ground and finally looked down at her parents, tilting her head slightly in loving recognition. Next, a large flare broke off from around her, reached down, and momentarily covered Randy and Natasha, gently pushing them to the ground. After the flare withdrew, they helped each other to their feet. Suddenly, the form that was once their daughter shrank to a dot and dispersed a powerful ring of life energy in all directions. The spectators quickly turned away as the edge of the ring harmlessly sped past them like a sonic wave. The hum stopped, and the blue dome began to disintegrate.

Thousands of light-blue flakes slowly drifted down like snowflakes, as if nature were gently apologizing. Reaching their hands into the air, dozens of spectators standing along the highway and others who had stopped their cars and gotten out tried to catch a flake before they faded away. Nova was gone. Her Papa and Mema, still facing each other, were dead. Dazed and traumatized, Randy and Natasha slowly walked over to their dead friends. Natasha slowly reached down and picked up Nova's necklace lying in the dirt between her Papa and Mema; then she burst into tears. Sirens could be heard in the distance, and good Samaritans rushed to help.

It took months before the area within a mile radius began to see some life again. Everything green had died that day, as did every animal in the area. All of them had their life energy pulled out by Nova. Dead trees and flowers were dead, and wilted leaves had to be replanted along the highway. But the massive brown scar of acres of dead trees and bushes can still be seen from the highway and the air.

The Department of Transportation had to put a parking area off the side of the highway because of the number of cars that always pulled over to look at the area's newest tourist attraction. In the gift shop, copies of videos taken by spectators of the incident could be viewed on monitors and were also for sale. Dr. Morgan's books and souvenir blue flake key chains were available. Snow globes, when shaken, offered blue glitter in light-blue water that gently fell on little trees inside. These were also for sale, along with shirts, coloring books, and other touristy items.

Margaret Stedman had the honor of publishing Nova's story in the LA Report from an exclusive interview with Randy and Natasha in her last edition as the editor before she finally retired. Before she left the newspaper, she added a dozen more framed articles on her wall from the trials of the politicians and military Officers involved with the five Casps.

Georgina decided it was her time to go as well. She had been with Margaret for many years and couldn't imagine working with anyone else. Her retirement will allow her to be more involved with her 'Advocates of Truth and Justice' brand, a hacking group.

Randy and Natasha struggled to live with the physical loss of their little girl and promised each other that they would have no more children of their own. They will always cherish their daughter's sweetness, love, and charm and forever be proud that even in her most profound sorrow and rage, she spared the lives of the drivers and spectators along the highway. She had thought to take their lives, but didn't. Her parents now knew that just moments before she vanished, their daughter, realizing that she had taken in too much life energy and wasn't going to survive, intentionally directed the single large flare to them. Not only did the flare increase the power of their abilities, but within the flare was Nova's essence. Since Randy and Natasha held hands when the large flare enveloped them, Nova was still alive within both of her parents, but was fully present only when they held hands. Their other promise to each other is that they'll never tell the media or the authorities.

Because Nova's essence was within them, Randy became even more brilliant with increased life energy. Natasha had even more life energy, thus having a more significant effect on nature. Together, they found they could control large amounts of life energy.

Natasha's Surprise Plan

Natasha and Randy sat in bed, propped on pillows, drinking wine. "You're quiet," Randy said. "What are you thinking about?"

"I'm so impressed that Nova spared the people along the highway."

"Me, too. She loved to save people," Randy replied.

Natasha continued, "Honey, you know she's still in us, right?"

"Yeah, I know. I sense her, too. Especially when you and I hold hands."

"Somehow, she transported her essence to us through the flare she directed over to us," Natasha said.

Randy replied, "I'm sure she did. It seems that we have her power, too."

"Want to hear something crazy?"

Randy took a sip of wine. "Sure. Why not? We're Caspers. Our lives are all about crazy."

"I'd like to start a business to teach people how to live a simple life by raising their food, making do, and being happier with fewer 'things,'" Natasha said.

"Will it mean that we have to move?"

"Yes, it does," she answered.

"So, where are you thinking?"

"It's a little place you might have heard of, Casper Island number five."

Randy reached over and took the glass of wine from her hand. "That's enough for you. There's nothing worse than a drunk, Casper."

"Imagine," Natasha said, "having our new home on the second floor and a gallery of soul-science history on the first floor."

"How about the business part?"

153

Natasha answered, "Casper Island is famous for its crime, mystery, and drama. We wouldn't have to pay much for marketing."

"Go on," Randy said.

"Paying guests could stay for a week in the houses and work. We'll all eat together in the pavilion. A Casper-styled life."

Randy handed Natasha her wine glass. "Sounds like you thought some things out. I guess it wasn't the wine speaking. If you can convince Charlie and Maria to help us, I'll look into what it will take to get to the island. I'll take some time, and it won't be easy."

Natasha replied, "They said yes. The island hasn't been touched since we left. The government will sub-lease it to us for next to nothing. We fly out on Friday to see it. More wine?"

Randy laughed as his wife took a sip of her wine.

Back on Casper Island 5

Randy, Natasha, Charlie, and Maria flew in a small float airplane to the island. It was the first time anyone had been to the mostly forgotten island, formerly referred to as CASP 5, since they had left over sixteen years ago. Natasha was the first one to notice that the buoys were gone. Through the window of the airplane, everything else looked about the same. The plane descended and flew just above the water before the pontoons scraped the water's surface. The pilot throttled back more and stopped as close as possible to the sandy beach.

"We should be back in a few hours, Nate," Randy told the pilot.

"Take your time. I brought my fishing gear and waders, so I'll be fine here on the beach."

Now that Randy and Natasha were standing on the beach, the changes were more than they had expected. There were just slight pieces of evidence that, at one time, a trail used to go up through the bushes and plants. Nature had almost retaken the island, but not the years of memories and emotions.

Walking up to the clearing would have been difficult if it hadn't been for Natasha extending her hands and using her life energy to push the bushes away gently.

At the end of the trail, they arrived at what used to be the thirty-foot space between the two rows of concrete houses. Small trees and bushes were spread out among patches of high grass, and a few wild chickens scattered into the underbrush. Two horses' skeletons, bleached by the Sun, lie next to each other.

"Chickens?" Randy exclaimed.

"They must be descendants of the original ones. They managed to survive over the years," Charlie said. "The houses still look solid. The roofs might need attention."

Looking toward the end of the clearing, Randy noted, "There's not much left of the pavilion. It would have to be rebuilt. The ruined piano sits under that large pile of old palm branches."

Charlie's slowly sweeping head stopped, and he pointed. "Maria, that was my house over there… Hey, Bear's bowls!"

The four walked over to Bear's food and water bowls in front of Charlie's old house. Lying next to the bowls was Bear's old buckled collar. Charlie picked it up.

"Bear loved everyone, but he was 'your' dog, Charlie," Randy said.

"Yeah, we were good buddies. He must have died here on my doorstep. I'll keep his collar and this water bowl."

Randy led the way to the brick fire pit. The red bricks were still in place, but the metal grate had rusted and fallen to the ground. Randy took the rusty poker and moved it through the ashes and dirt. He reached in and pulled out a hardened glob of plastic when he felt what he was looking for.

"Anyone remember this? It's the cell phone that Margaret gave me after I went to her office. We never had to use it."

"So many memories of conversations and meals with friends," Natasha said with a grin.

"Randy, I'd like to go inside my house."

"Sure. Let's walk over."

Randy took the doorknob and pulled at the front of what used to be Natasha's house. The rusty hinges resisted with a long squeak. The

155

four of them entered the house and were immediately greeted with a musty smell. The small bed was still made and orderly. Natasha touched the green plastic chair. The candles and magazines were still in their places on the small desk. Her old clothes hung on the wooden rod in the makeshift closet. The others continued to watch as she opened and closed the three drawers in her small dresser.

Natasha noted, "Everything is still in place but covered with almost seventeen years of dust and time."

They left and pushed the door closed as Randy thought out loud, "I wish Dr. Morgan were here. I wonder what he would say."

Charlie walked over to a spot in the clearing. "Maria, this is where we made the first Caspers ring."

"And the second one was next to it," Natasha added.

"This is also where Randy beat up an armed guard. Randy, remember Jim? Igor? That guy never liked us."

"Hold on there a minute," Randy exclaimed. "This is also the place you punched an Army Lieutenant in the nose! Pow! So, your assault outranks mine!"

After they all laughed, Natasha said, "Alright, you cowboys. Let's show Maria where the garden is."

The group found the overgrown trail and took it to the garden area. "Weeds," Randy said. "Hey, there are still a couple of squash plants growing."

Maria pointed. "You've got some raspberries too."

Natasha stepped into the old garden and hummed. The garden faintly hummed back. As she approached, the raspberry bushes leaned toward her, and the leaves of the squash plants turned up to her.

"That's amazing," Maria said. "Charlie told me all about what happened here, but now I see it with my own eyes. Natasha, I've got an ivy plant that's not doing well. Do you make house calls?"

Natasha answered, "Sure. But my charge for a house call is a standard hot cup of tea. Where would you like your new house to be?" She pointed over to an area in the trees. "I'm thinking about building our house back there. The first level will be a gallery dedicated to the history of soul-science."

Randy said, "We'll build a house for you wherever you want. And on the beach, we could build two replicas of the cargo crate number 5."

"With the secret compartments, right?"

"You better believe it," Randy replied, smiling.

"About the gallery, I think I can still remember where I buried your scuba gear. We could also put it in the gallery, along with Bear's bowls and collar."

Randy held out the melted cell phone. "And this, too."

Natasha replied, "Great! You two take all the time you need to consider joining us here now that you've seen what it will take to get this up and running again."

"No pressure," Randy added. "Just know that we can't do it without you."

Natasha gently pushed Randy. "Honey, stop! That's not fair."

Charlie looked at his wife, who smiled and nodded in response. Charlie smiled back. "We're in."

Aside from the faded paint on the small houses and a few missing shingles, most of the houses were in good condition. Pieces of dried kelp were evidence that, over the years, waves were forced up to the homes. The storage building's door was still closed, continuing to hold supplies of rusting canned goods stacked on the shelves. Mice had chewed the books into small pieces. The community center had taken the worst from time and the winds. Most of the walls of thatching and the roof had gone, but the slanted bamboo structure was there. Time and weather had slowly destroyed the piano. Remaining strands of old red paint that had survived the years of rain and sun sat loosely on the top of the picnic tables, but the brick fireplace fought and won the long assault, except for the rusty steel grate.

"Well, it's ours now," Natasha said.

"It feels so much different," Randy replied.

They agreed to rename Casper 5 to Morgan Island and placed the name on a nice sign on the dock.

Charlie and his wife Maria gladly accepted the invitation to return to the island and manage it. They insisted on living minimally and built a modest house near the gallery. Natasha finally persuaded them to have solar panels for electricity.

Fourteen months later, two number 5 model cargo crates rested on the beach as part of the theme for the forthcoming tourists. A small dock was built to accommodate passengers who would fly in. Randy and Charlie were able to place new buoys around the island, marked 'Private Island.' There were solar panels on the roof to provide electricity to the upstairs residence where Randy and Natasha lived. The first floor below them was used for the gallery, where pictures and various items from that time were displayed. Videos of Nova and the wolves, as well as the ring of life energy in the median between the north and southbound lanes of the highway, were available to view on wall monitors. Georgina anonymously donated her radio to the island. The underwater propeller and scuba gear Randy used to return to the island were also displayed. A small spotlight was kept on Nova's necklace as it hung behind security glass next to a series of large pictures of her at different ages. A portrait of Dr. Sydney Morgan, for whom the island was named, hung above a special plaque that told the story of the activist and friend he was. Nothing was for sale, and donations weren't solicited. The four Caspers decided the gallery would not double as a retail store. They felt it would cheapen the value of the memories of those who had passed and the movement to protest the science.

Eventually, small charter airplanes with water pontoons left from the southwest coast of California to take visitors directly to the island's beach. For a week, tourists got to stay in the houses and live the rustic way the Caspers had. They all understood it was a work vacation where they would be assigned a chore or two upon arrival. They got to do everything that the Caspers did. It was part of the experience that most visitors were glad to accept, along with the 'one person to a house' rule, working with strangers, using the crude toilet, taking showers outside with cool to warm water, and gathering to eat their meals at the restored community center, where friends were made. The tourists also understood that once they arrived, they couldn't leave until the three days were over. Finally, their cell phones and all other electronic devices were held for them during their stay. These rules helped instill in them just a small degree of what the Caspers had to manage for over a year. When each tourist left, they were given a t-shirt that read, 'Morgan Island' on the front. Below that, it was written, "I Survived Morgan Island #5."

One of the favorite times for tourists was when it became their turn to place their hands on Natasha's shoulders as she walked through the garden, singing her beautiful melody. The guests felt the life energy flowing through them and were surrounded by the hum from the plants that leaned toward them. Afterward, they selected ripe vegetables and fruit they needed for meals.

Charlie led a team to feed the fish in every water pen, from the mature ones to the fingerlings and fries. If it was on the menu for the evening meal, they netted fish for dinner. Of course, the tourists had to clean and prepare them.

Maria brought the guests to collect eggs, milk the goats, and care for the two horses. The original animals were left behind the day the Caspers were taken back to the mainland. Recently, some of the remains were found scattered around the island. The most heartbreaking discovery was the remains of the community's pet, Bear. He wasn't permitted to leave the island with the Caspers. It was Lieutenant Witherford's revenge for being humiliated the day they all left. To some people, a pet could never be replaced, but Randy and the others enjoyed his new German Shepherd, Beartwo, in honor of the first Bear.

Tsunami!

No one was upstairs near the radio when news of the earthquake at the bottom of the sea, miles away, was announced, and the subsequent tsunami warning was issued. But Charlie did notice that the water level on the posts at the fish farm was dropping quickly.

"Let's get back to the community center right now!" he ordered the three tourists working with him. "I think we're about to get a lot of water!"

They all scrambled back up the trail. Charlie shouted the warning to Maria and her helpers at the goat pen. Maria directed her guests to follow her to the pavilion as Charlie ran to the garden to alert Natasha and her helpers.

When Randy was finally warned, he ran upstairs to his house and turned on the radio. A twenty-five-foot wall of water was rushing toward them from the southeast and would be there in about fifteen to thirty minutes. There was nowhere safe to go and no way to get the sixteen people safely off the island in time.

Randy just informed everyone gathered at the pavilion that the tourists were terrified. He lifted his hands to still the crowd. "I need your attention! Quickly! Listen. Natasha, Charlie, and I are going to the beach. We hope we have enough power to help. Now, you can stay here or come to the beach with us, but there's no safe place."

Natasha and Randy followed Charlie down the trail to the beach. Beartwo followed. The water had receded significantly. The frightened tourists followed behind them, talking among themselves in panicked voices. It was hard to imagine that the beautiful day would face the dark side of nature in just minutes.

Two minutes later, one of the tourists holding binoculars yelled, "Oh my God! I see it!" On the horizon, a very high wall of water was approaching. Beartwo looked out to the water and barked. Some panicking tourists tried to climb palm trees at the beach's edge while most others ran back screaming to the residence and waited on the balcony.

Charlie looked at Randy and Natasha, "We must try. We take a stand right here." He offered his hands. The three of them formed the Casper circle as Maria stood by. Immediately, the hum began. The vibration was strong enough to cause the top of the sand around them to dance. The Caspers had never felt this amount of power before. A light-blue ring formed above them, but it was much thicker than before, turning the penetrating sunlight a deep blue. Excited strands of colors swam inside and formed a moving woven pattern—next, the massive blue dome formed around the whole island. The ominous wave was determined to wash away the defenseless, screaming tourists and ruin the buildings. Moments later, the twenty-foot-high wall of rushing water smashed against the dome and splashed white foam high into the air. Raging seawater piled up against the dome and wrapped around it, but the water didn't get through.

Charlie excitedly exclaimed, "I can't believe that just the three of us generated enough life energy to do this!"

"No, Charlie. There are four of us here," Randy said, smiling.

"And the fourth person might have more power than the rest of us combined," Natasha added. "Nova is here too! We'll explain later."

"I can't wait to hear about that!" Charlie said, surprised.

Everyone stayed put as the water level above them slowly subsided. When the water finally returned to an average level, the Caspers decided they could let their hands go. The ring of life energy and the massive blue dome disappeared as the tourists who fled to the pavilion and those who climbed palm trees returned to the beach.

Later, the last small amount of water rushed up on the sand toward the group of nervous tourists who screamed and ran. They started laughing with relief as the little wave gently withdrew back into the water before it reached their feet. Everyone was still excited and relieved as they returned to the pavilion.

Randy went back upstairs just as the Coast Guard was on the radio, calling to see if there were any survivors, and was surprised to hear a reply from Morgan Island.

"We're fine here," Randy explained. "We had some water come up into the treeline, but there was no real damage except to our dock."

He lied about the dock. The tsunami never touched it, but he felt he had to give some bad news to avoid drawing any more attention.

"Ok. I don't know how you were spared, but we are glad to hear it. Some of the other islands weren't so lucky."

"Thanks for checking in on us, though. We appreciate it," Randy replied.

The next day, the tourists gathered on the beach with their bags. Two small airplanes tied to the dock waited to take them back. One young man named Jer took Randy aside.

"I broke a rule, and I'm sorry."

"How's that, Jerry?"

"When I arrived, I didn't turn in both of my cell phones. I videoed the tsunami on the phone; I was hiding. I can't tell you how badly I want to save the video after watching it over and over last night, but I want to forward it to you and erase it from my phone. There's a lot of trouble around Casper things, and I want no part of it."

"You didn't send it anywhere, did you?"

"No, Sir. I did not," Jerry promised convincingly after he showed Randy his 'sent' messages.

"I appreciate that. Could you send it to me right now? And for your honesty and good deed, you and a friend are invited to return for another three days on me. The only condition is that the video doesn't get out. But please bring just one phone next time."

"Wow, thanks! There's a creepy image of a girl inside the dome with her arms spread toward the wall. She slowly turned her head, glanced at your group, then up at the tsunami as it hit."

"I'll look at it," Randy promised with a shrug. "But sometimes clouds and waves can randomly take the shape of familiar things." Randy stayed calm on the outside, but inside, he was anxious to see if the image was his daughter.

That evening, Randy, Natasha, Charlie, and Maria were upstairs in the residence, standing around talking before having dinner.

"So, Randy, do you want to tell me about the 'fourth' person in our circle on the beach?" Charlie asked.

Randy looked at Natasha. "Honey, maybe you can explain it better and show them."

Natasha walked over to the TV monitor and turned it on to watch the video of the tsunami. She started the video, let it play, and paused it at the point just before the wave hit the dome. She touched the screen and said, "Look right there. What do you see?"

Maria answered, "That's crazy. It appears to be a young woman standing there with her arms out, her palms facing forward. It looks like she's pushing something."

"That's because a young woman was standing there. That's our daughter Nova. That's her hair and her shape," Randy said.

"And," Natasha tapped the pause button until the image of the girl turned to the side. "that's the profile of her face."

Randy took Nova's framed picture off the wall and handed it to Charlie, who looked at it and then compared it to the image on the video as his wife looked over his shoulder. Charlie put his hands up in front of him. "Woah. As a Casper, I've seen a lot of strange things, but are you telling us that Nova is… still here?"

"Exactly," Randy replied. "She transplanted her essence into Natasha and me before disappearing the day the Morgans died. Do you recall the flare that appeared in the video? We feel her, and sometimes we can even hear her. But we've never actually seen her until this video."

Maria took her hand from over her mouth. "Oh, my word. But what are you going to do? Every one of those tourists is telling the story about the tsunami and the dome as we speak."

"Yeah, we know. Natasha and I talked about stopping the tourists from coming until things settle down."

"Hey, let's suspend the tourism, and why don't you two take a little vacation? Get off this island. Maria and I can handle everything."

Natasha looked at Randy. He saw in her eyes that it was what she wanted and needed. She nodded slightly. "Okay."

Dark Chapter

Randy and Natasha held hands as they walked down the sidewalk in the Los Angeles shopping area. "I love our island home," Natasha said. "But after a while, I started to get that island fever."

"Me too. Charlie and Maria are taking care of things. We are on vacation. They can go when we get back."

A young woman walked by them, passing about a foot away. A light-blue flare jumped from Natasha to the young woman, who stumbled slightly with a brief look of confusion. She turned around and stopped. Randy and Natasha also turned to look at her with an unexplainable feeling. The young woman stood smiling at them.

"Mommy and daddy..." Randy and Natasha just stared at her. "It's me, Nova!"

Natasha looked firmly at her and said, "Whoever you are, that's not funny. It's mean and cruel."

"You still have my necklace from Papa and Mema. You showed Charlie and Maria the video of the tsunami. You saw me."

Randy pushed his head slightly forward. "Nova?"

"Yes. It's me! Aren't you excited to have me back?!"

"My God," Natasha quietly exclaimed. "What did you do?"

Randy looked up and down the sidewalk. "Come on. Let's step into this pizza shop."

Randy ushered them to a table, where they all slid into a booth. Natasha was teary-eyed.

"I had to," Nova insisted while drying her tears. "I want to be part of my family again. I want my life back."

Randy asked, "How is the young lady in there?"

"She's fine," Nova answered dismissively.

Natasha reached over with her hand and placed it on Nova, saying, "Nova, we're so happy that you're back... But you know it can only be for a short time. Right?"

"I know, Mom. But I just wanted to see you and Daddy and 'talk' to you... and be alive again." Nova cried.

"Who is she? Randy asked.

"I don't know."

Natasha asked, "What's her name?"

"I don't know. She's about my age and resembles me a bit. That's why I picked her. I can look deeper inside her if you want to know."

"Hmmm, we have a situation to figure out. Baby, you must let her go. We'll figure it out. Okay?"

"Daddy, it's lonely when I'm inside you. I can feel you, but I rarely hear you, and I can never talk to or see you or Mommy."

Natasha gently said, "Honey, you should... come back with us for now."

"Ok. I'm sorry. I thought you would be as excited as I am."

Randy and Natasha placed their hands together. A light-blue flare jumped from the young woman back to Natasha, who quickly got up, walked out of the restaurant, and hurried down the sidewalk with her husband.

The confused young woman awoke in the booth, sitting alone. She looked around, wondering how she got inside a pizza place.

"What would you like to drink?" the server asked, standing there and looking at the bewildered young lady, who glanced around and left without saying a word.

Stepping around the corner of a building, Natasha held Randy as he closed his eyes and shook his head. They began to walk without holding hands until they found a park bench to share.

Natasha said, "Ever since Nova left that young woman's body, she's been restless. It's like being pregnant and feeling her move."

"I can feel that too, and she won't be content to be inside us anymore."

"I wish we could help her. What will we do if she does that again, Randy?"

Randy shrugged his shoulders. "Try to talk her out of it again if we can. If we can't... I don't know."

"It seems if we don't hold hands or touch, she can't leave. But is this how we want to spend the rest of our lives? Keeping the door locked so our teenage child can't get out? We can't touch each other when other people are around?"

"For now, Randy."

Randy and Natasha casually walked through the aisles of a department store, inspecting different items. The middle-aged store Manager walked over and stopped.

"Are you all finding everything all right?"

As Randy and Natasha turned to talk to him, their shoulders accidentally touched. A light-blue flare jumped from the Manager. He looked disoriented for a split second, then turned away and ran down the aisle. "Mommy and Daddy, don't try to stop me!" he shouted.

Randy and Natasha ran after him out of the store and followed him down the sidewalk.

Some people quickly stepped aside for the Manager, and he knocked into others who dropped grocery bags and coffee cups. He tried to run across the busy street but got hit by a car and rolled to the opposite curb next to a gray-haired older woman standing on the sidewalk. The older woman leaned over the store manager, lying on his back.

"Young man, are you okay?"

The store Manager suddenly opened his eyes and looked at the older woman. A light-blue flare jumped from him to the senior woman who stumbled before shouting to Randy and Natasha across the street, "I'm going to live again!"

"Nova!" Randy shouted. "Stop!"

The older woman dropped her cane and struggled to run away as fast as she could, as the wounded store manager sat up and looked around in confusion at the crowd that gathered around him. Randy and Natasha ran after her.

A block later, the senior woman stumbled and dropped into a parking lot, her hand over her heart, as a young man slowly rode past her on a bicycle. He saw the older woman on the ground, stopped, and began to dismount. A light-blue flare jumped from the older woman to a young man who tried to steady himself for a moment, then pedaled quickly away, shouting to Randy and Natasha, "I must! Go back! Leave me alone!" The young cyclist quickly pedaled out of sight into the bustle of the streets as Randy and Natasha ran and stopped, gasping for breath, as people gathered around the older woman. A man who was giving her CPR as a teenager called 911.

Natasha was almost out of breath. "We lost her."

Randy replied, "She's hurting people. We must find her."

At the busy outdoor Farmer's Market, a row of small vendor booths bordered the sides of the parking lot. Shoppers walked around from booth to booth, inspecting and buying vegetables, candles, fruit,

166

jars of honey, and other items. Randy and Natasha arrived and slowed to a walk.

"She's here. I can sense her," Natasha said, trying to settle her heaving breathing.

They walked into the crowd, carefully looking at each person. Natasha gestured for Randy to stop beside a woman with a baby stroller who was buying vegetables from a vendor at a stop.

Natasha looked at the woman. "Nova?"

"Excuse me?" the woman answered as she looked at them.

"Sorry. We're looking for our daughter," Randy offered.

"Well, I'm flattered that you think I look young enough to be your daughter, but you have the wrong person."

"Sorry," Randy said.

Nova slowly looked down at the toddler in the stroller. The toddler looked up at her and began to cry. "Please stop trying to find me. You don't understand!"

The surprised mother looked down at her toddler and knelt. "Oh, my God! Did you hear that?! She talked in sentences! Wait till your daddy hears about this!"

Suddenly, a light-blue flare jumped from the toddler to the closest shopper in a wheelchair. She quickly pushed her way through the dense flow of pedestrians. The flare left her, then skipped across the heads of the people in the crowd, slightly stunning each person who looked around in confusion.

"Come on," Natasha said. "This way!"

Randy and Natasha walk quickly, weaving through the crowd to follow the flare through the Farmer's Market and toward a construction site.

Three construction workers wearing orange vests and hard hats were hosing down the side of the cement truck parked at a deep, partially filled form with vertical rebar.

Natasha whispered to Randy as they approached, "She's here, in one of these men."

Randy started the conversation. "Hi, guys. We're looking for our daughter."

167

One of the workers said, " I'm sorry, but you can't be here. It's a dangerous area."

"We haven't seen anyone," the second worker said.

The third construction worker ignored them and wouldn't even look. Natasha walked over to him. "Honey, we love you and just want to help. Come back. We'll figure it out."

The construction worker began to cry and slowly backed up. "You can't! There's nothing you can do! I'm staying in this body for as long as I need to!"

Tripping backward, the construction worker fell into the form and was impaled on standing rebar. His body slid down to the wet cement. Natasha screamed. A light-blue flare from the construction worker reached out and withdrew as the body flailed.

"Mommy! Daddy! Help me!"

Randy shouted, "She's too far away from anyone! She can't transfer herself!"

The first construction worker held him back as he desperately looked for a way down into the form. "Hey! Stay back! That'll happen to you, too, if you try to go down there!"

"I'll call 9-1-1!" the other worker announced as he quickly took out his cell phone.

Natasha pointed her hand down to the form and concentrated. The construction worker's body, covered in wet cement, slowly began to rise through the rebar. A light-blue flare shot into the air from the body, desperately searching in vain for someone to attach Nova's essence to. A small light-blue dome formed above the form, then disintegrated into hundreds of light-blue flakes that fell and disappeared.

Natasha cried, "We lost her! Our Nova is gone!"

Randy hugged his wife as tears ran down his face. "Baby, I'm so sorry! Let's go home."

Back Home In Casper 5

Randy and Natasha stepped through the Gallery of Soul Science door on Morgan Island and slowly walked around. Randy flipped the lights on. Gentle music began to play, spotlights came on, and videos played on the wall monitors. Under spotlights on the floor, Randy's scuba gear was on a mannequin and roped off beside one of the original picnic tables and Casper's green, plastic chairs. Under other spotlights on walls were Bear's collar with his name tag and bowls, the melted cell phone from Margaret, a large group picture of the Caspers with Bear taken from the laptop's camera the day they left the island, and framed front pages of newspapers from the LA Report. Every item had a brief sign explaining its purpose. Copies of Dr. Morgan's books opposing soul-science: 'Sorrow from the Soul,' by Dr. Sydney Morgan, 'It's Us, Julie,' co-authored by Dr. Morgan and Julie, and 'Casper's Plight,' co-authored by Dr. Morgan and Randy Dickensen, were sitting upright on floor displays. Several wall- monitors looped videos of the two Casper's rings, Nova in the wolf exhibit, the aerial view of the car accident scene where the Morgan's died, the tsunami, Dan and Jody who anchored the reports when the Caspers were returning on the Coast Guard ship, and the construction site video where Nova died.

Nova's tribute bust, wearing her necklace, sat on a pedestal anchored to the floor with a lovely plaque that read: "Nova Dickensen, A young woman in whom the life-energy of nature itself took residence in a heart so pure and kind."

A tribute plaque under a large portrait of Dr. Morgan gave a condensed version of his involvement: "Dr. Sydney Morgan - Both father and adversary of the science of the soul. He discovered the soul and rejoiced. He touched the soul and wept. He protected the soul and fought."

Charlie, Maria, and Beartwo arrived at the open door a few minutes later. "You guys, okay?" Maria asked in a low tone.

Randy and Natasha turned to look at their best friends. "Yes. Come in."

Charlie added, "We just want to know if we can do anything."

"Oh, you're both so sweet," Natasha replied. "But we're fine."

Randy said, "I think it's about time we re-open Casper 5, Morgan Island, to visitors. What do you think?"

"If you two are ready, so are we," Charlie answered.

Maria smiled and nodded.

"Have you heard the news yet?" Charlie asked. "Just came out."

"No," Natasha answered as she and Randy stood attentively.

Maria explained, "Dr. Brown is going to prison for a long time. The senators testified that even though they approved the funding of the ASP, they didn't know about the cruelty or mental illnesses. They claimed that the only deaths they knew of were the ones that had been reported in the media."

"The senators, however, are not off the hook completely. They're in trouble for not managing the ASP and for blindly approving the funds without accountability," Charlie added. "They also claimed not to know the Casps. They left no trail for the investigators to find any connection."

"At worst, they'll get censured," Randy said before pausing and slowly looking around the gallery. "We've won some battles, and we've lost more often. But the soul-science has stopped. I guess that means that we won the war."

"We did win, so come on; let's open this island for business. We have a lot of people who are very excited to stay with us!" Natasha said as she cheerfully led her husband and their best friends out the door.

Randy, Natasha, and Maria walked out the door. Charlie turned out the lights, closed the door, held Maria's hand, and they walked away.